THORN OF VIOSKA
A VALKYRIE BESTIARY TALE

BY KIM MCDOUGALL

Published by WrongTree Press.
Editing by Elaine Jackson.

Paperback ISBN: 978-1-990570-45-2
eBook ISBN: 978-1-990570-44-5

Version 1

FICTION / Fantasy / Urban
FICTION / Fantasy / Paranormal

Author's Note

Thorn of Vioska is a companion novella to *Worlds Don't Collide* (Valkyrie Bestiary Book Nine), written from Emil's point of view. While it is a stand-alone story, the events take place during the same time period, and there will be spoilers included for *Worlds Don't Collide*. I suggest reading all nine books of the Valkyrie Bestiary first, and consider this one as a *digestif*.

This one is dedicated to all the Inbetweeners.

PROLOGUE

June 2054

They caught Tereza while she slept. Stupid. So stupid! She should not have given in to exhaustion. She should have kept going, perhaps fed more often to gain energy, even if she had to drink rats.

She should have run.

But there was the child to think of. He could not drink blood yet. He needed milk from her body to survive. And he was so little. His stomach couldn't hold a full day's sustenance in one meal. She'd tried to slow her pace to feed him, but he fussed. Her little Janzek knew his own mind, and he didn't like to feed on the run.

So she'd stopped. She'd found a hollow behind the root ball of an upturned oak tree and hid as well as anyone could in the menacing forest.

The baby's warm body fit into the crux of her elbow and breast like a missing puzzle piece. He kneaded her flesh with tiny fists and made small, contented noises as he swallowed. It was those noises that did her in. First they captivated her, then they lulled her.

And then she slept.

She woke to a bruising grip on her shoulder and Janzek's cry as he was jostled out of his comfortable dreams.

They put her in a cage.

"Please!" she pleaded. "Don't take us back. He will take my child! Please, for the love of your own mothers, please don't take us back to him!"

The opji guards ignored her. They were all strangers. Ichovidar had made sure not to send anyone who might be sympathetic to her cause.

They walked through the whole night, heading east, back the way she'd come. Her cage was little more than a box and it hung on two long poles carried by four opji. It jostled and swung in a sickening rhythm and Janzek would not settle. He cried for hours.

Eyes appeared at the tiny window in her box.

"Shut that child up or we will." The guard pounded on her box with a fist.

Tereza spat through the window. The eyes disappeared.

They would not dare to hurt her or the child. She was Ichovidar's toy and anyone who touched her would pay for that pleasure with his life.

It was small comfort.

During the day her captors set four wojaks to guard her cage while they slept. The others guarded against attack from the forest.

And Tereza plotted. She tested all the seams and joints of her prison, looking for weaknesses. She would break free. She didn't know how yet, but before they reached Vioska, she would find a deficiency in the guards or the cage and she would exploit it.

Because she was never going to be under Ichovidar's control again. She would kill herself first—and her son—before she let that monster take them.

When the sun set, the guards picked up their poles and her cage began its lurching progress toward Vioska and her fate.

Hal limped down the drive toward the homestead. The air felt thick in his lungs and he wheezed as his feet sloshed through one puddle after another. Even the recent rain didn't mask the smell of burned wood and flesh. And sure enough, when they rounded a bend in the driveway, they found a pile of blackened foundation stones in place of the old farmhouse. Smoke rose in anemic wisps from the fallen roof.

Hal tipped his head from side to side as he surveyed the damage. Bones crackled in his neck. Gods, he was getting too old for this kind of business.

It was the third burned out homestead they'd investigated in the last two days. He'd told the Queen to send a younger man, but she insisted she needed someone with experience, and someone she could trust to bring back the truth. And Hal had never been able to deny Leighna anything. That's why she was queen. The weight of her stare was enough to make a man change his mind. And if she smiled, well, you might as well put aside all your plans because you were going to do whatever she asked.

"Take two men and scout the barn and other outhouses," Hal said. "I don't want any surprises."

Sergeant Heath nodded and left with his men. Hal ordered others to go through the ruin of the house. His team included several imps who were great at getting into small spaces and an ogre who could lift an entire wood truss by himself. Hal had handpicked the team. It also included four elves from the old court—two trackers and two archers—and a squad of beefy trolls. They knew what they were up against and they were all ready to fight.

Leighna's last words came back to him. "There are rumors of a new vampire king in Vioska. A mage, by all accounts. He seems a bloodthirsty sort." She'd smiled. "Or more bloodthirsty than usual. There are rumors that he's raiding homesteads scant miles from the ward. I want to know if this is true. And I want to know why."

And so she'd sent him on this scouting mission. Almost immediately, Hal had found evidence that the opji weren't just raiding farms and feeding off the homesteaders. They were taking them. For what purpose? He didn't know, but he had suspicions, and none of them were pleasant.

Hal cracked his neck again. His jaw ached, probably from sleeping on the hard ground for days at a time. He left his patrol to do their work and found a spot to sit and fill his pipe.

Farshell, one of his imps, found him smoking while he sat on an overturned barrel outside a cow shed.

"Anything?" Hal asked with the tip of his pipe clenched between his teeth.

Farshell didn't bow. No one bothered with formalities like that in the Inbetween.

"Nothing. No bodies or even bones. That house was empty when it burned."

Hal took a last draw on his pipe, then tapped out the ashes.

"Any signs of a struggle?"

The imp made a face. On anyone else it might seem like a sneer, but Hal had been working with Farshell for over twenty years, and he recognized it as the imp's thoughtful look. He was trying to work out a problem in his head.

"Might be," he said finally. "Found some broken dishes, and Axel thinks he smelled blood."

"A bit of blood and a broken plate don't necessarily add up to a fight."

"Nah, it don't." Farshell shrugged. "But Axel swears the blood is human, and there was lots of it. Mostly burned off now."

Axel was their shapeshifter. His wolf's nose was rarely wrong. He would be able to smell the blood even under the damp ash.

Hal slapped his thigh with a palm. The tobacco had perked him up. Time to get moving.

"Call the others back. We're leaving." They had a dozen more homesteads to check on before he could return to the Winter Palace with his report.

The following week went much the same. As their list of homesteads dwindled, so did the spirits of Hal's squad. At each farm, they found much the same: burned farmhouses, abandoned livestock and no homesteaders. Whoever was raiding and taking captives wasn't even trying to hide the signs of their passing.

Hal's elf scout, Ginny, easily tracked the passage of a large group heading into each farm, then away from it. Presumably with captives. It wasn't clear to him if the same raiders were going from farm to farm, or if this new opji king had sent out multiple squads.

And still the question nagged at him. Why would the opji take so many captives? Food was the obvious answer. The opji fed on the blood of humans and fae. And beasts when they could get nothing else.

In his long career as Captain of the Queen's militia, Hal had seen more than his share of opji attacks against homesteaders. In 2036, the opji made it all the way into Barrows, the shanty town north of the city. Hub was in its infancy then, and the vamps slaughtered over a hundred people before a force was put together to stop them. Hal had been part of that force, and it shaped his career. Ever since, he'd thirsted to stamp out opji incursions whenever they flared up.

But this…

He stared at yet another burned out farmhouse, yet another abandoned farm. This wasn't a typical assault. Vamps didn't take captives. They attacked.

They fed. They disappeared. They didn't leave a trail of gratuitous destruction in their wake.

The opji were up to something. As he sucked in smoke from his pipe, Hal vowed to discern the logic behind these attacks and bring that news home to lay at his queen's feet.

By the last homestead on the list, Hal could no longer sit in his saddle. The constant jostling of the mare's stride had woken a deep, throbbing pain in his back. He rode on the bench beside their quartermaster as they headed to the last homestead on his list. The hard bench wasn't much better than a saddle.

Hal grunted and shifted his bulk, trying to find a comfortable seat. There was none.

It was near dark when they rolled down the drive. Hundred-year-old pines lined the road, towering above them and blocking the last light.

"Something's not right," Hal mumbled.

"Sorry, sir? Did you say something?" The quartermaster leaned in.

"Stop the wagon!" Hal's chest felt tight, like the weight of an impending doom sat on his lungs. He stuck his fingers in his mouth and whistled. His next breath came with a wheeze.

One of the elves wheeled his horse around and trotted back to the cart, his face creased with concern. "My lord?"

The silence of the forest had alerted Hal. That and the creeping sense of unease he'd been ignoring all day. One of his sergeant's joked that Hal had a spidey sense, in homage to an old cartoon. And it might seem like science fiction, but his instincts had kept him alive, and he'd learned not to discount them.

"Call everyone back," Hal rasped. The elf looked stricken. "Do it now!" The elf responded to the command like he'd been whipped, turned his horse, and galloped up the lane.

But it was too late.

The unnatural silence was broken by screams as the opji attacked.

HAL SURVEILLED THE DEAD. Six opji, a dozen stinking wojaks and two of his squad—Omma, one of his trolls and an imp named Kez. All would be buried. He wouldn't risk sending smoke signals with a fire.

Ginny stood with him beside the bodies.

"These aren't the raiders we've been following," she said, confirming what he was already thinking.

"The tracks from the last homestead were at least two dozen on foot, plus a wagon. A big one. These guys came in from the east."

"A different raider patrol?"

"Maybe." Ginny chewed on her bottom lip, holding back the obvious question. If these were the raiders, where were the homesteader captives?

Hal gave her his thanks.

"You should get that looked at, my lord." She nodded toward his left shoulder. His shirt sleeve was soaked in blood. But with all the other aches and pains in his body, he barely noticed the wound.

"I'll be all right." He smiled. "What's one more scar on this old hide, eh? And who would have thought an opji could shoot an arrow anyway?"

Ginny's face scrunched into a frown. "It was a surprise, my lord. Perhaps they are adapting to fight us on our own terms."

"Hmm. Perhaps." It wasn't an idea he wanted to consider. The opji had always fought like the animals they were, with tooth and claw. If they'd decided to pick up weapons, they could become a real threat.

What was this opji king up to?

"My lord!" Sergeant Heath called as he trotted back down the lane. He wasn't even out of breath when he caught up to them. "My lord, you'll want to see this."

The box was a four foot cube strapped to sturdy poles for carrying. A small window opened on one side. Hal peered through it, but saw only darkness. Then the shadows shifted and eyes appeared from the gloom. Huge, dark eyes in a pale face.

"Please, take me…" The voice was soft and breathy. "Please." Fingers gripped the edge of the window. "Take me to Montreal. Take me away from *them*."

A baby mewled and a sound of relief went through his squad. At last! They found some of the captives!

An imp moved to open the latch on the box, but Hal stopped him.

"Show me the child." His voice was harsh, and he sounded like a commander, even if he knew his body was failing. The woman in the box moved away from the window. A moment later, the pale light shone on the face of a baby.

Hal's spidey sense told him everything he needed to know.

The woman and child were opji. He studied the box, shone a light inside. It was cushioned for comfort, but locked from the outside. There was no mistaking that the woman was a prisoner—a prisoner, but an important one. Her captors had taken pains not to hurt her.

"Please." The single word leaked out of the box like a sob.

Hal made a singular decision. There hadn't been an opji inside Montreal's ward for nearly twenty years. But whatever was so important to this new opji king, would be important to Queen Leighna too. He would bring her the opji woman and child.

But first he'd have the surgeon fix up his wounded shoulder. It was starting to ache.

LEIGHNA HELD THE LETTER from Lord Lughwaite in shaking fingers. She read its contents twice before lowering it to stare at Hal's dead, gray face.

His sister, Imogen, had thrown herself over his chest and wept. Leighna wished she was a mere lady-in-waiting too so she could indulge in grief. Hal had been her best commander and a friend.

But she was queen. Always. And she had duties to fulfill. She turned her gaze toward the woman clutching a fussy baby. Her name was Tereza, or so she'd said. Leighna didn't trust anything that came from opji lips.

"Why were you being held by your own people?" she asked.

Instead of answering the question, Tereza knelt like a supplicant.

"Please give my son sanctuary and I will tell you everything you want to know about Vioska and Ichovidar."

Leighna considered the opji woman. She was extraordinarily beautiful even with matted hair and dirt smeared across her face. She had dark eyes with thick lashes in a pale, heart-shaped face. She claimed she'd fled Vioska to protect her son, Ichovidar's son.

Now she stared up at Leighna with a seemingly guileless plea in her eyes.

Leighna spoke quietly, a trick she'd learned in Parliament. A quiet voice was one that expected others to listen to it.

"You will tell me everything you know about your people. About Vioska, this Ichovidar who calls himself king. Everything. I want to know about your religion, your language, your feeding habits. I want to know how you weave your clothes and sweep out your houses. Everything."

Tereza nodded.

"And then, I will consider what to do with your child. What is his name?"

"Janzek." The woman bowed her head. "His name is Janzek."

Leighna touched the sleeve of her lady-in-waiting. Imogen raised her head from her brother's body.

"Imogen, please take Janzek and see that he is fed and bathed." That would give the woman something to fuss about other than her dead kin.

Imogen Lughwaite wiped her eyes on her sleeve and approached the opji captive. Tereza squeezed her child to her chest and he let out another hearty wail.

"Your son will be cared for, as long as you cooperate," Leighna said.

Tereza nodded and sniffled. She handed the bundle over.

Imogen tucked the baby into the crook of her elbow and cooed to him in a singsong voice.

Leighna pinned Tereza with on of her best royal glares and pointed to a chair. "Now sit and talk."

Tereza slumped onto the chair.

Over the next hour, Leighna would learn the surprising and devastating details of the opji's new *Gazgroda* policy, or what Tereza translated as the Holding. Their new king wasn't just taking humans. He was breeding them!

Leighna glanced at Hal's gray face. He had given his life to bring her this news, but to what purpose?

She would have to alert Parliament, but already Leighna knew the ineffectual machine of politics would take months, if not years, to digest this information. And then they would probably do nothing.

Homesteaders weren't Montreal citizens after all.

In her small suite in the Winter Palace, Lady Imogen Lughwaite bathed the baby with a soft, warm cloth. He watched her with enormous eyes. She grabbed one of his flailing feet and kissed his toes. The baby cooed.

"Such a pretty boy with precious little toes. But what an improper name! Janzek? Whoever heard of such a thing?" She paused and frowned, but contrary thoughts didn't last long in the lady's head and she smiled again. "No, Janzek won't do. I will call you…Emil."

November 2, 2084

Emil had ridden with Raol before, but he didn't know him well. This trip wouldn't bring any enlightenment about his character. His guide was not one for idle chatter. In fact, the only time he spoke was to warn Emil of some pitfall or incoming creature.

Raol rode with a modified saddle that was little more than a thick leather pad strapped to the horse by a girth. His pony was well trained to the reins, and he had no need of stirrups that his short legs wouldn't reach.

Raol was a ratatosk, a sentient squirrel creature who stood about three feet tall. He wore a leather vest and a belt with a knife. His tail rose behind him like a fluffy question mark. A small saddle bag with a bedroll was tied to his saddle. Emil thought it remarkable that the little creature could survive alone in the Inbetween with so few provisions.

They'd been on the road for only one day and already Emil missed the comforts of home.

Yesterday, they'd mostly ridden in silence. This morning, they had enjoyed a cold breakfast of water from a nearby stream, then mounted and turned the ponies east. Next to the taciturn guide, Emil had been lost in his own thoughts. As they grew ever closer to Vioska, those thoughts were turning into fears. To put them aside, he tried to strike up a conversation.

"So you're from Asgard. What's that like?"

They rode side by side. Raol never stopped scanning the shadows under the trees like a nervous bird.

"It's much like this. Many trees."

"Do you have family there?"

"No."

"Do you like it here, on Terra, I mean."

Raol's tail swished. "Yes."

"And the Inbetween doesn't scare you?"

He turned slightly to look past Emil's shoulders. "No."

Emil gave up. Conversation with Raol was like trying to pull a flame from a fire.

They rode all day, stopping only to water and feed the horses. When the sun was more than halfway toward the horizon, Raol held up a paw.

"What is it?" Emil probably spoke too loud. Raol made a *zzzt* noise that Emil took to mean, "Shut the hell up."

A coy-bear cub tumbled into the path ahead. Uh-oh. Where there was a cub, there was a mama.

Coy-bears were a post-Flood War creature. Kyra told him they either came through a rift in the veil or they'd were a mutation caused by all the left-over magic in the Inbetween from the thousands of bombs dropped during the war. Either way, the cub was deceptively cute, black and roly-poly with pert ursine ears and paws, but the longer snout of a dog. A full grown coy-bear could take down a horse.

The cub sat on its butt and lifted a foot in the air, examining the toes as if it had never noticed them before. A second cub hopped out of the trees and landed on its sibling. Then Mama lumbered into the path.

Raol sat perfectly still. Emil handed him the reins to his mare, and jumped down. He walked toward the coy-bears with his arms outstretched. Wasn't that what you were supposed to do? Make yourself look bigger? Or were you supposed to lie down and play dead? Emil could never remember. He opted for looking menacing as he crept toward the bears.

Mama stared at him for a long moment, trying to decide if he was food or danger. Her top lip rolled like a wave from one side of her mouth to the other and a deep grumble emerged. Emil froze. The bear was so close, he could see the individual whiskers on her muzzle.

She lunged toward him in a feint, then slipped into the trees. The cubs followed.

Emil felt his blood pound in his veins and realized he was terrified. It was amazing! And the first time he'd felt anything but grief in months.

He returned to the horses and mounted. Raol's expression was guarded, but then he was a squirrel, and they didn't have particularly expressive faces.

Raol waited another minute until the sounds of cubs crashing through the underbrush faded, then urged his pony on. The horses seemed unfazed by the encounter, but Emil was sizzling with nervous energy.

"That was amazing! Those bears were like ten feet away!"

"Mmm," said the ratatosk master of discourse.

"I mean how often does that happen? What are the odds?"

"Quite good, actually. And if you're not quiet, those odds increase tenfold."

"Wow. You said a full sentence. Good for you."

Raol turned dark eyes on him. He was possibly trying to glare, but the effect was diluted by whiskers and fluffy ears.

"What?" Emil held up a hand. "I'm just saying, you're not the most chatty guy I've ever met."

Raol cocked his head. "Do you hear that?"

Emil listened. "The bird? Yeah, I hear it. Why?" He'd been listening to the gabble of some kind of duck for a while.

"That's a sandhill crane calling its mate. They are more than ten miles away."

"So?"

"So sound carries in the forest. There are creatures here that can pick up your chatter from a mile away. Not to mention your scent."

"My scent? What's wrong with the way I smell?" Emil sniffed his armpit. Sure, he hadn't showered in two days, but he couldn't smell that bad yet.

"You stink like the city," Raol said. "Like pavement and electricity."

"I didn't realize those things had a smell."

"They do. And to prey animals they smell like food because they mean you don't know how to survive in the forest."

"Huh." Emil had gone through his whole life with everyone around him smelling like food. And now he was the prey to an unknown menace. It was an uncomfortable feeling. He shifted in his saddle. That was getting uncomfortable too. His mother had made sure he could sit a horse and look good doing it, but jumping poles in a ring was a far cry from hours of plodding on a trail. He was going to have sores.

Another creeping and disagreeable thought came to him. Maybe this wasn't such a good idea. Maybe charging headlong into the Inbetween looking for opji was actually the dumbest thing he'd ever done.

Was he doing it because Kyra asked? Because the thought of losing Gabe still brought him awake most nights in a panic? Partly. Maybe. It went deeper than that. His hand strayed for the crutch tied to his saddle behind him.

Kyra needed information on the opji if she was going to defeat them, and he'd volunteered to get that information. Gabe had been a sacrifice in this growing conflict. And yes, Emil wanted to make those opji bastards pay for it. But he'd agreed to this foolhardy mission for another reason.

It was time for him to go home, to learn where he'd come from.

The forest trail emerged into a stretch of grassy field and Raol picked up the pace. Emil dug his heels into his horse's flanks and trotted toward his fate.

THEY DIDN'T BUILD A fire that night. Raol was content with a cold meal of nuts and dried berries from his pack.

Emil hunted. It had been years since he'd relied on game to feed his bloodlust. During his teen years—when his desire for human blood became overwhelming—he'd often escaped the city for days at a time to hunt in Dorion Park. He'd sated himself on the blood of rabbits and deer and gone home exhausted but with a quieter soul. Until the bloodlust drove him mad again.

These forests were ripe with rodents of all kinds. He let a red squirrel dash by without chasing it, thinking that Raol wouldn't like to know he'd eaten his kin. But rabbits were fair game, and plentiful. When he'd had his fill, he washed blood off his face and hands in a small stream and returned to camp.

Raol's tail snapped back and forth when he approached.

I guess I don't smell like pavement anymore.

He was full of energy now and didn't want to hunker down and sleep.

He paced a few steps to the left and returned to the small clearing, then went right. Back and forth, never diving deeply into the forest that was now inky black. Raol watched him with ears flattened to his head. The horses pranced nervously every time he swished by them.

Emil finally stopped and rounded on the ratatosk.

"What is it?" he hissed.

"You make too much noise."

"So what? So the opji hear us. That's what we're trying to do, isn't it?"

Raol bared small, sharp teeth at him. "There are worse things in these woods than vampires."

"Right." He was being an idiot.

He flopped down beside Raol, then reached over to grab the crutch from beside his saddle bag. It was long enough to fit snugly under his arm when he stood and made mostly from a new hawthorn branch, except for the top foot. That was old wood, blackened by many hands. Oscar, the alchemist who'd made it for him had stained the newer part. It was a very good match, but if you ran a thumbnail over it, you could feel the seam between the two woods. The head of the original staff was hidden under a new block with padding to fit his underarm, but if he plucked off this cap, it would reveal a brass eagle with a wicked beak and talons gripping the shaft.

Emil twisted the shaft and the wood parted at the seam. A long silver blade slid out. The Thorn of Vidar, a relic as mysterious as it was deadly. His sensory magic was nothing compared to Kyra's keening, but even his skin crawled when the blade was revealed. He had the odd sense that it lusted for blood as much as he did.

He ran the blade along his forearm, drawing out a red line. Before the cut healed, he scooped up a drop of blood and smeared it along the blade. Instantly, the creeping shivery feeling subsided.

"How often must you do that?" Raol had curled himself around his pack, but his eyes and ears were still alert.

"I'm not sure. We didn't have time to test it." Emil shoved the blade back into its wood sheath.

Kyra had brought him to Oscar Lewis's lab where the old alchemist hooked him up to a thaumagauge and tested the efficacy of the thorn's magic. When sated with his blood, the thorn cast a glamor over him, making him appear to be human. Even Kyra's hyper-sensitive keening hadn't been able to see through the disguise. They'd estimated the range of effectiveness to be about five hundred meters, but they had no idea how long the glamor lasted, so he blooded the thorn every day.

"How can you be sure the opji will let you keep it once you're captured?" Raol asked.

Emil grinned. "I can be very persuasive."

In truth, the question bothered him. The whole mission hinged on Emil getting inside Vioska. Without the thorn, the opji would sense that he was an aberration—a vampire who'd never undergone the zycha rite—and kill him on the spot. He had to go in as a captive, find out everything he could, then escape and bring his news back to Kyra.

So she could kill all the opji.

He lay down with the crutch cradled in his arms, but it was a long time before sleep overtook him.

RAOL HELD UP A fisted paw. It was his signal to stop and be quiet. His ears perked forward and his tail had gone from question mark to exclamation point.

They'd been on the road for an hour. Shadows under the trees were just beginning to lighten. Raol jerked his paw. They left the road—which was hardly more than a deer track—and pushed the horses into the forest. Ten steps into the trees, Raol stopped and turned his pony. Emil never saw the command, but the animal spun its hindquarters and stood still as a statue. Even its tail didn't swish.

Emil didn't bother to try and turn his mare. They didn't have the same connection as Raol and his pony. The mare barely tolerated his commands and enjoyed testing his limits by snapping at saplings and stamping her feet. But even the mare sensed the tension in the air. Instead of tramping through the underbrush and alerting whatever it was that had spooked Raol, the mare froze with her nose inches away from the pony. Her eyes showed white, and Emil could feel her muscles bunched, ready to leap away.

Steady, old girl. He brushed her shoulder with his hand and projected calming thoughts at her.

Voices filtered through the trees. Emil turned and his saddle creaked. The voices hushed. Minutes later, a group of humans came up the road on foot. Raiders or possibly displaced homesteaders.

Emil watched their shadows pass and thought—raiders. Homesteaders would have a cart or at least packs. These people were wary, and walked with swords ready. They carried no packs other than belt pouches. That meant they had a camp nearby.

They waited in rigid silence while the raiders passed, then waited another five minutes to be certain they didn't double back before Raol nudged his pony forward. Emil yanked the mare's attention away from some late season sumac and followed.

The morning was turning bright, but the light seemed brittle, like it might crack at any moment and let in a storm.

A man appeared on the road. Raol's pony shied and backed into Emil's mare.

The man pointed a dagger at Raol's chest.

"Yer gonna give me those horses. And yer weapons." He flicked the blade. "Now."

The guy made a good show with the menace. He was black-haired with a shaggy beard and prominent yellow teeth. When he smiled, he gave off rabid dog vibes.

Emil gave him a seven out of ten for effort.

The mare's ears twitched, but he'd already heard the other raiders come up behind them. They'd circled back to spring a trap.

"Now, get off the horse and toss me the reins," Blackbeard said. Emil wouldn't have been surprised if he finished his threat with a hearty, "Arrrrg." At least he didn't lie and promise not to hurt them. Everyone on that road knew there was about to be violence.

Raol didn't move, except for his tail that quivered like electricity ran through it.

Emil plucked the crutch from his saddlebag, jumped down and sauntered up to Blackbeard like they were just two friends meeting on the docks. He leaned heavily on his crutch, and the man's eyes were drawn to it.

That's right. Nothing to see here but a frail refugee and his walking stick.

"Hey, friend, you don't want to do that." Emil nodded toward the blade that caught the light flickering through the canopy.

"Do what?" Blackbeard glanced sideways where a second raider emerged from the trees. Another man and a woman blocked the horses from turning. Four raiders. He had to assume there were more hiding in the trees.

"You don't want to stick me with that," Emil said.

The man grinned and leaned forward. "I think I do."

Emil was four feet away now. Just short of the raider's reach. He raised his voice. "You don't want these horses or our weapons. You don't even want our blood because it will come at the cost of your own. Turn around and leave before—"

"I'm going to kill you," Blackbeard snarled.

Emil lashed out with the crutch and rapped him on the face. Blood burst from the raider's nose.

"Ah, ah." He waggled his finger in front of the bloody mess. "I wasn't finished talking yet. As I said, turn around and…oof!"

The raider slammed into him, drove him to the ground and jabbed the blade into his neck.

Emil gaped up at the crazed eyes. Blood filled his throat and he willed himself not to choke.

The man's breath reeked of rotting meat. Blood dripped into his mouth from his wrecked nose and stained his teeth red. He grinned, clearly thinking he'd won this contest.

Emil showed off his fangs and plucked the blade from his neck. The wound was already healing.

Now it was the raider's turn to gape. Emil leapt on him like a cobra striking. His teeth closed on flesh. He ripped a chunk of flesh from the man's throat and spat it aside, then rose, displaying bloody fangs for the benefit of the others.

Blackbeard flopped on the ground, his hands pressed to his throat as he tried to hold in his lifeblood.

Emil spat on the ground. "Yuck. I've got beard stuck in my teeth." He grinned at the second raider standing some ten feet away. "Now, are you going to try your luck too?"

The man shook his head. He was already backing away. The others melted into the trees like they had never been there. Blackbeard died choking on his own blood.

Emil sloshed water over his face from his canteen.

Human blood. It made his teeth sing. It hummed through his veins like a drug, and he'd only swallowed a drop.

Oh, what it must be like to live on such a cocktail.

He wiped his face on his sleeve and went looking for his horse. The mare had been frightened by the scent of blood but he found her a hundred meters down the road where she'd been distracted by a crabapple tree that still hung onto its fruit. He pulled off a few apples and tucked them in the saddle bag for a treat later and mounted.

Raol waited for him beside the cooling raider.

His tail twitched. "You are not afraid to die." Emil grinned thinking it was a compliment, until Raol added "That is foolish."

"Whatever." He dug in his heels and the mare loped ahead. He wasn't going to let some imperious little rodent harsh his buzz.

THE FIGHT WITH THE raiders left Emil feeling empty, like someone had pulled a plug and let all his blood drain away. He'd have to feed again soon. And the bloodlust made his thoughts turbulent.

Who was he to think he could fool a whole city full of opji? What did he even know about them? The last time he'd been in Vioska, he'd been in diapers. They could all be sorcerers with the ability to see through the thorn's glamor—to see through the ruse that was at the core of his very being.

Near sundown, Raol veered off the road and they made camp beside a narrow stream. Someone had built a shrine nearby, a stone fountain that caught water in a bowl for easy drinking. Thunder rumbled somewhere far away.

Emil unsaddled the mare and hobbled her where she could graze on late grasses.

"I need to hunt." He turned his back, almost wishing the ratatosk would tell him to be careful or go quietly or some other unnecessary admonishment that would show they had even the smallest connection. Kyra would have done it. But Raol was silent.

Emil didn't bother with stealth as he ran. The ground was covered with damp leaves and rain drummed down, masking the sounds of his steps.

Bare branches grabbed at his sleeves as he flew through the forest. The uneven ground betrayed him, turning his ankle. Pain shot up his leg and still he ran. Physical pain never lasted.

He ran so far that he feared he wouldn't make it back to Raol. Then he ran farther, until a stitch in his side bent him over gasping. He dropped to the wet leaves and curled into a ball. Rain fell in hard, wet pellets like it was trying to crush him into the earth.

He lay there for hours. The rain finally stopped. He felt battered. And cold. Inside and out. Just as he had since the moment he'd learned of Gabe's death.

Finally, gnawing hunger pulled him out of his stupor.

He rolled and put a knee under himself, then pushed up to standing. He swayed. A rabbit wouldn't do tonight. It was time to hunt for something bigger.

He found the stream they'd camped on and washed off the blood. He'd left the body of the gumberoo for the scavengers. Vultures and litches needed to eat too. Fresh blood in his veins soothed the storm inside. If he didn't get into another knife fight, he'd be sated for at least a week.

He followed the river downstream. It was part of the watershed that would eventually run into the great Ottaway River—the river that flowed down from Vioska. He couldn't be sure how far he'd run, but his feet were already wet, so tramping through the stream seemed like the safest bet to finding Raol again.

The rain had stopped, leaving the night eerily still. Mist draped around tree trunks. Emil stopped with one foot raised and ready to splash into the water. He put his foot down quietly and crouched.

No, he wasn't hearing things. A voice came through the mist from up ahead, low and curt like a command.

They were probably camped by the stream too. He'd be visible even in the near darkness if he tried to sneak past them. He left the stream bed and hiked up a slope, but curiosity kept him close. The voices came again and he crept forward until he spied smoke from a guttering fire. Crouching on a bramble-covered rise, he watched.

Four opji sat around the fire. They were easily recognizable by their dark uniforms that made them look like nineteenth century undertakers. Ridiculous. The entire opji culture needed a good fashion overhaul.

Emil scanned the small camp. Where there were opji, there were wojaks.

He spotted six of the aberrations placed strategically around the camp.

They crouched in the mud with their arms wrapped around their shins. He would love to learn the secret of how the opji controlled the mindless creatures.

Another small sound caught his attention and he spotted a wagon nearly invisible in the gloom on the far side of the camp. The horses had been left in their traces so they could only graze on the meager scraps at their feet. The wagon bed was a large box. From this angle he could see one barred window on the side. Fingers wrapped around the bars. A face appeared, young, dark-skinned with large frightened eyes. The kid clung to the bars, but he wasn't crying. That sound came from within the cage. For that's what it was—a cage full of human captives.

He'd found the opji who were rounding up homesteaders.

RAOL WASN'T SLEEPING WHEN he returned to camp. The ratatosk was up and ready with his knife drawn.

"Were you followed?" he asked as he scoured the shadows between trees for whatever creature that made Emil run.

"No. I found them. Opji raiders not five kilometers from here." Emil untied the Thorn of Vidar from the saddlebag, took a canteen and a knife and hung them on his belt. He turned to Raol with a grin.

"Do I look human?"

Raol cocked his head like a bird sizing up a worm. "Too much tooth."

Emil lost the smile. Opji fangs weren't much more than sharp canines, and he'd long ago learned the art of hiding them.

"Better. But still too white. Opji white. Like your skin has never seen the sun."

A growl rumbled in Emil's chest. "I don't have time for a tan."

"Rub dirt on your face. You're too clean anyway."

Emil grabbed a clump of dirt and smeared it through his hair, then dragged dirty hands over his face.

"Better," Raol said. "Do something about the leg."

Right. They'd already discussed this. In order to keep the crutch, he had to convince the opji he had need of it. They wouldn't want to carry a wounded man. Luckily his shirt was blood-stained from the fight and the hunt. He stripped it off and tore it into a bandage that he wrapped around his shin. He drenched the clean shirt from his pack in the river and through the mud before wringing it out and putting it on. Leaning heavily on the crutch, he squinted one eye and jutted his jaw as if he dealt with immense pain.

"Much better." Raol nodded.

Remembering Blackbeard, Emil said, "I feel like a pirate. Arg! All I need is an eye-patch."

Raol didn't answer and he wondered if they had pirates in Asgard.

Now that he was leaving, he found he would miss the little rodent.

"Take care of my horse, right? Make sure she gets back home. And tell Kyra…" He wracked his brain for something witty and meaningful to say. And got nothing. "Just tell her I'll see her in the spring."

"May the All-father bless your passage."

"That sounds more like last rites than good luck."

Raol twitched his tail. "There are many kinds of passages."

"Right. Well safe travels to you too. And don't eat any mushy acorns or whatever." He hoisted his small pack over his shoulder and headed upstream.

The sky was marginally less gloomy, and with the canniness of most night walkers, he gauged that sunrise was about an hour away. When he neared the opji camp, he feigned a limp and started crashing through the underbrush like a coy-bear drunk on fermented apples.

That ought to get their attention.

Stumble, crash. A loudly whispered curse.

Within minutes he was surrounded by snarling wojaks.

3

The wojaks circled him like snarling hounds until two opji stepped through the trees. One pointed an old-fashioned revolver at him.

Isn't that cute?

Emil forced back a smile. He tried to cower. The shaking legs were real enough though. Turns out that fake-limping was exhausting.

The second opji held a long metal rod. He gestured with it. When Emil didn't move, he stepped forward and jammed the rod against his shoulder.

Pain fired through him. It hijacked his nervous system. His arms seized, back arched, knees buckled. He lost time and found it in the dirt, with his face pressed against the ground.

"Get up," said a heavily accented voice. Emil braced himself with one palm and pushed.

"Leave your weapons," said the opji.

Emil's fingers fumbled to unclasp the belt with his knife. It fell to the ground. His fingers closed over the crutch and he leaned on it as he stood.

The opji menaced him with the prod again. "The stick too."

Emil raised his free hand. "Please, I can't walk."

The prod lunged for him again, but stopped just short of his chest when the second opji snapped a command. The two men exchanged words in the guttural opji language. Emil could only pick out a few. He heard the name Ichovidar once and *krowa*, which he knew was the name given to the captive humans the opji kept as breeding stock.

While the opji argued, Emil kept his head bowed and studied them from under lowered lashes.

The one with the prod was young. He had a prominent brow that overshadowed the rest of his face. The other one was older, leaner and obviously used to being in charge, though the younger opji seemed to be looking for an excuse to challenge that command.

Finally, they came to a grudging agreement. The younger opji jabbed him once more in the shoulder but didn't activate the electrical shock. It was the peevish shove of a child who didn't get his way. Then he stalked off.

The other opji assessed him. "Were you shot?"

Emil shook his head. "It's an old wound. From childhood." He didn't need to pretend to stumble over his words, not when two wojaks were snarling at his back, hungry for his blood.

"He wanted to kill you." He nodded toward the trees where the other opji had disappeared. "But Alain is young. Impatient. He does not see the big picture. My name is Teo. You belong to Vioska now. Do you understand?"

Emil nodded like someone too frightened to speak.

"Good. You can keep your crutch, but know it cannot hurt me or any opji. And if you try, we will feed you to them." He waved his gun at the pacing wojaks.

Emil nodded again.

Teo motioned him forward. Emil leaned heavily on the crutch as they tramped through the trees. Alain had obviously washed his hands of the whole affair, but another young opji joined them as they reached the camp. She opened the door on the wagon. Emil pretended to look around like he might bolt, then saw the wojaks ready to give chase. He gave a shuddering sigh and climbed into the wagon.

The smell hit him first—unwashed bodies, shit and sick in a small space. Then his eyes adjusted and he saw the people. A family was huddled in one corner, parents with their grown children. The boy he'd seen through the bars sat in a corner with the head of another man in his lap. A brother or father. The man's eyes were closed. He was too still to be asleep, but his chest rose and fell, so not dead either.

The door slammed shut and Emil limped into the small space. The box was too small to stand in, and there was no place to sit that wasn't covered in filth, so he crouched.

No one spoke. Minutes later the wagon lurched, and he fell against the wall. He sat and tried not to think of the things seeping through his pants.

Mentally, he put a check mark beside mission part one: get captured.

THE ROAD TO VIOSKA wasn't a smooth one. The wagon bumped and swayed and jolted along a narrow trail. Emil stopped trying to brace himself for each impact. His bruises would heal, unlike the other captives in the box.

One of the women in the family group cried nonstop. No one consoled her. Perhaps her family had given up trying. He noticed another person he hadn't seen at first arrival. A woman lay on the hard floorboards, her eyes closed—asleep or dead.

The young boy he'd seen through the cage bars stared into the dark with wide eyes. The older man rested with his head in the kid's lap. His nose was obviously broken and his bottom lip scabbed and swollen. Blood crusted over a cut on his hairline. The guy had taken a beating.

"Is that your dad?" Emil asked.

The kid shook his head. "My brother."

"I'm Emil."

"I'm...Stephen. This is Raymond. Ray. He's my brother." The kid didn't seem to notice that he'd already said that.

Maybe he's in shock.

Ray moaned and started to gag, then to vomit.

"Roll him!" Emil shot forward and pulled Ray from Stephen's grasp, turning him on his side before he choked.

Ray's stomach was empty and he only upchucked a bit of mucus.

"He's going to die, isn't he?" Stephen's bottom lip quivered.

Emil thought it was a miracle Ray was still alive, but he said, "Nah. He looks like a tough guy. Did he hit his head?"

"I don't...I don't know. He told me to run and...and I did. But They caught me. He...Ray was already in the wagon when they put me in here. I didn't see...I mean, he could have hit his head. Do you think? Oh, my god. He *is* going to die."

The kid was full on crying now, like a harmony to the woman sobbing in the front corner.

Ray moaned again and his eyes opened. He looked right at Emil.

"You opji?" His voice rasped.

Emil felt a shiver of fear and delight go through him. Maybe it was his injury, but this man saw right inside his soul.

He laughed. "'Course not. Just a schmuck who let himself get captured. I'm Emil." He held out a hand to shake. Ray took it. The gesture was strangely intimate in the small dark space.

"Guess we're all schmucks." Ray pulled himself upright and leaned against the wall. He put a shaking hand to his head where the hair was crusty with dried blood.

Hours later, the wagon stopped. The family shuffled away from the back door, and the woman's sobs wound down to hiccups.

The door opened. Sharp morning light cut across Emil's eyes and he shielded them. When he looked again, an opji stood in the open doorway with two wojaks at his back just in case anyone got the urge to run. Emil recognized Alain from the night before. The young opji hefted a bucket into the wagon bed, sloshing water over the side, then slammed the door shut.

The father of the family grabbed the bucket. He was a skinny guy, with the memory of a full head of hair clinging to his skull around his ears. He dipped his hand in the water and sucked at his fingers. When he'd had his fill he let his wife and children drink.

What an upstanding guy.

When the whole family had drunk their fill, except for the dead or unconscious aunt, Emil waited for the bucket to be passed on. The man saw him watching and pulled the bucket between his legs.

"Hey Dad, you going to share that?" Emil pointed to the bucket with the end of his crutch. The man hugged the bucket to his chest for a minute, then shoved it forward.

"Good choice. You're a generous man…?"

"Brian," said the man.

"Brian." Emil smiled. "You're a credit to your family, Brian." He hooked the bucket with the crutch and dragged it toward Stephen.

He nodded. "Go ahead."

Stephen drank from his cupped hand then fed water to Ray before looking up expectantly at Emil. There was less than an inch of water left in the bucket.

"Finish it," Emil said. "I'm okay for now."

Stephen lifted the bucket and drank again, then helped Ray to finish the dregs.

The wagon rolled on. Ray watched him in the dark.

The next time they stopped, the light was fading. Emil didn't recognize the opji at the door.

"Bucket," he snarled. The empty bucket was passed forward until it reached him. Only then did the opji dump a fresh one inside. He glanced toward the sleeping woman in the corner. He leaned in a sniffed the air, then slammed the door. A moment later, it opened again. The opji held a cattle prod ready. The family shied away. The mother shrieked. Emil didn't know how she still had the energy for it. She'd been crying all day.

A second opji jumped into the box. He hissed in disgust at the smell or because his foot slid on shit. He grabbed the unconscious woman by the feet and dragged her out.

Mother shrieked, "Please, she's fine! Don't take her!" The cattle prod flared with a sizzling zap and the woman fell to the floor, convulsing.

Emil pushed forward and the opji lashed out with the prod. Emil dodged and it struck the side of the wagon. He jerked the vamp's arm backwards until it snapped. The prod fell to the dirt outside the wagon. Beside the old aunt's body.

Emil yanked the broken arm behind the guard's back. The opji screamed. The wojaks on guard snarled and suddenly there were three more opji in the small circle of light around the wagon.

Everyone froze.

Emil and his whimpering opji captive filled the entire doorway of the wagon.

Teo stepped forward, his hands held in front of him in a placating gesture.

"You cannot escape." Teo had a sibilant lisp and he drew out the word "escape."

Emil jerked the broken arm and the opji yelped. "I'm not stupid. I know those wojaks would tear me to pieces within seconds. I just want to talk."

Teo studied him for a long minute.

"Talk, human."

"You obviously don't want us dead or you'd have killed us already. I'm guessing you have a quota for bringing in new krowa. Am I right?"

Teo's lips twitched, but he didn't respond.

"So if you don't want more of us to die, we need food and more water. And we can't stay locked up in a box filled with shit. Humans aren't like opji. We're weak." He smiled and twisted the arm again. "But if you treat us with just a bit more care, we'll all live to fill out your quota. You'll roll into Vioska with a full load of healthy krowa, instead of half dead meat for the wojaks. Which one do you think Ichovidar would prefer."

The vampire king's name produced the desired effect. Teo's pupils dilated. Another opji snarled and stepped forward. Teo held him back.

"You are smart for a human."

Emil grinned. "We're not all dumb asses. And we're not all weak." He gave the broken arm one last twist then shoved the vamp out the door. He landed face first in the dirt.

Emil stepped back into the shadows of the wagon. This was the moment of truth. Teo would either order him killed or he'd listen to his suggestions.

Teo snarled a command over his shoulder and a moment later, a second bucket of water was hoisted into the wagon. The door slammed shut.

Snarls and growls of feeding wojaks filled the night. The opji wouldn't let the old aunt's blood go to waste.

The family huddled around their bucket. The mother sank to the floor. Silent. She was finally out of tears.

The wagon rolled on.

Brian spat on the floor between Emil's legs. "Stupid. You could have got us all killed."

Emil turned away to show the old man he didn't fear him.

"I thought you were brilliant," Ray said. He was propped against the wall and the dim light shone on his feverish forehead.

Emil smiled. "Thanks." He laid a hand on Ray's brow. It was hot and clammy. Ray took his hand and held it in his lap. Then he closed his eyes.

The wagon rolled on.

Ray slept leaning against the wall. His head bumped it with each jostle of the wagon. Emil didn't understand how he could sleep through that. The kid had laid his head on Ray's lap and curled up like a kitten.

Humans were adorable when they slept.

A bump in the road tossed Ray sideways. His head fell on Emil's shoulder. He didn't wake. His broken nose whistled. Emil carefully touched his forehead again. It was even warmer. One of his many wounds was infected.

Ray moaned. Emil squeezed his hand.

Hold on, buddy. Just hold on.

Emil spent a long night staring at their clasped hands as they headed toward Vioska.

Teo personally escorted them to their new home. Guards opened the gate on a huge pen. The humans inside automatically stepped back. They knew the drill.

Brian's family—minus one aunt—filed into the pen first, followed by Stephen, then Emil with Ray leaning heavily on his shoulder.

"Welcome to Krowa Pen Five," Teo said. "It's got a beautiful view of the Hall of Mages." He said it without a smirk. Was Emil imagining things or was Teo more resigned than happy about his job?

Ray staggered toward the open gate, but Teo stopped him. "Not you." He nodded to a waiting guard. "Take him to the infirmary."

The gate slammed shut.

"Ray!" Stephen stuck his small fist through the chain links, reaching for his brother. The retreating opji ignored him.

Then they were alone with the krowa.

"Come on." Emil took Stephen by the shoulder.

"Will they kill him?" The kid sniffled.

"I don't think so. They would have done it already. I think they're going to make him better."

"They'll try to heal him, if they can. If not, they'll turn him," another krowa said.

Emil turned to examine their welcome wagon. The guy leaning on the fence had once been beefy, and even though his frame was wasted from time in the krowa pen, he still had the calm arrogance of a big guy.

"Turn him into what?" Stephen said.

"Never mind." Emil gave him a gentle shove toward a group of kids squatting in the dirt and haggling over piles of rocks. "Go introduce yourself."

Stephen shrugged and wandered off. Emil was continually amazed by the kid's resilience. During the long ride to Vioska, Stephen had regaled them with made up stories about superheroes. He said he wanted to be a comic book artist when he grew up. Looking around the krowa pen, Emil thought that future was looking kind of bleak.

He leaned on his crutch and turned to their greeter.

"You must be the sheriff in town."

The guy crossed his arms and frowned. A thick reddish beard covered most of his face, and his hair was too long. He'd been in the pen for a while.

Emil tried again. "I'm Emil."

"Liam." He didn't offer a hand to shake.

"That's Stephen." He gestured to the kid. "So what's the deal, Liam? Are they going to bleed us, fuck us, or feed us to the wojaks?"

Liam continued to study him in silence. Finally, he pushed himself off the fence. "The deal is, you behave. Don't cause any trouble. Don't touch the women unless they ask. And maybe you'll live through the night."

He turned away and disappeared into the ranks of huddled men and women.

"Nice guy," Emil said to no one in particular. He scanned his new home.

The pen was a long narrow cage. One side butted against a stone wall with an overhang that jutted out twenty feet. The rest was open to the sky and the elements. Six cast iron wood stoves were spread along the length of the pen and provided scant heat. It was only November, but temperatures already dipped below freezing at night. The krowa huddled together with only ragged blankets for warmth. Most of them were too skinny and Emil wondered how they would survive the coming winter.

He moved into the pen, looking for a spot to settle down. Stephen was already deep into negotiations over his own pile of rocks, but for Ray's sake, he would keep watch on the kid.

The novelty of new arrivals wore off quickly and most of the krowa went back to staring into space. Some paced. One painfully thin man sat with his arms around his knees, rocking and mumbling. His eyes were glazed as he stared at something the rest of the krowa couldn't see.

Emil fake-limped to the corner farthest from the gate and sat next to the fence, staring at the town beyond. Then he started counting opji.

AFTER TWO DAYS IN the pen, Emil had a better idea of how things worked. A few of the krowa kept to their family units. They took their rations and stayed out of trouble. Among the others, fights broke out often. They were near silent squabbles, usually over a loaf of bread or an extra bucket of water. Liam broke these up before the guards noticed. A stocky man named Neil acted like the sheriff's deputy. But where Liam was forceful and fair, Neil seemed to take pleasure by getting in a few hits with the brawlers.

Emil decided that Neil was dangerous and tried not to gain his attention.

When food was dumped into the pen on the second night, a fight between two women became heated. One woman screamed when the other punched her in the face. She reacted by yanking out a hunk of hair from her attacker. Then things got really messy.

The guards came in with their prods and zapped people randomly. Convulsing bodies hit the floor as the opji moved through the crowd toward the fighting women. They were zapped again and again until they lay unconscious in puddles of their own piss.

The guards left them there.

"It could have been worse," Liam said. Emil hadn't heard him approach. He was too stunned by the casual brutality he'd just witnessed.

"Worse?" He schooled his expression to neutrality.

"Fighting isn't tolerated. If they were men, they'd have been fed to the wojaks. "

Emil nodded.

The krowa talked. He'd heard that young, healthy women were favored by the opji. They were given extra food and water. Sometimes a pretty one would be plucked from the pen and never seen again, presumably to become the play thing of a rich opji. The others were left to fend for themselves with the hopes that they would take up with one of the male krowa and breed. Most of them did. Lying awake at night, Emil heard the unmistakable sounds of pleasure and release all around him.

During the day, Emil stood by the outer cage wall, watching the town and getting an estimate of opji numbers. Most of the daily activity centered around the massive hall facing the pen across the wide square. There were barns close by. He could smell the distinctive tang of manure, and twice he saw teams of horses being led through the streets.

Vioska wasn't a pretty town. The Hall of Mages was the only ornate building he could see, and even its decoration was stately rather than pretty, with large columns flanking two massive doors. Stone steps led from those doors to the square where on most mornings opji soldiers came out to exercise and practice combat.

Wojaks roamed the town too, but never alone. They were always magically tethered to an opji herder. Emil could just spy a wojak pen in the far corner of the town square, but the creatures inside huddled in the dirt and he couldn't get an accurate count. He supposed there had to be more pens elsewhere too. His fingers tightened on the chain links. He needed to get out of this cage and look around. Until then, he watched and he listened. He even added to his scant opji vocabulary.

The hall was called Mago Noka, so he assumed "mago" was "mage." He heard that term in hushed conversations too, especially when a group of opji came out the massive doors of the hall to watch the soldiers training. Emil looked for a white-blond head that could be Ichovidar, but the mage king never appeared.

Several times, he spotted Teo among the soldiers practicing in the square. Once, he caught him looking toward the pen and their eyes locked. Emil willed him to come nearer so they could speak, but Teo looked away. The next time he came out, he ignored the krowa all together.

Emil couldn't help thinking that Teo wasn't like the other opji. He'd shown them only the barest hint of mercy on the journey to Vioska, but that was more than the other opji had done. And he'd seen something in his eyes. Recognition? That was probably wishful thinking. If they suspected he was anything but human, he'd have been taken away by now. No, he'd seen something else in Teo. Fear. And once he figured out what frightened Teo, he could press that pain point.

The guards brought Ray back on the third day. As soon as they dumped him inside the pen, Stephen ran to prop him up. Emil hobbled over, a bit too fast for someone sporting a limp. Ray swayed on his feet. His fever was gone, but he was weak as a coy-bear cub, and his dark skin had a sallow tone. Emil tucked his shoulder under Ray's arm and they hobbled to the bit of ground space they had claimed.

"Let me help you," Liam took Ray's weight.

"Thanks." Emil didn't want to let Ray go, but he had to remember the limp.

Stephen chattered about the people he'd met in the pen, and the food, and how he'd collected stones that could be gold from the gravel around the pen's door with another boy named Freddie. Ray let his brother ramble, clearly used to the kid's chatter.

"Freddie's calling you," Emil finally said. It wasn't exactly true, but Freddie was looking at them curiously, and he figured that was about the same thing. Stephen glanced worriedly at his brother.

Ray waved him off. "Go. I'm gonna sleep." Stephen dashed off to find his friends.

Liam left Ray sitting with his back against the stone wall.

The space Emil had staked out for him and Stephen wasn't one of the best in the pen. The warmth of the last wood stove barely reached them here, but Emil had noticed a definite pecking order among the krowa. You either took the spots by the fire by force or you earned them. Emil didn't mind earning his spot since he didn't much feel the cold, but for Ray and Stephen he'd think about forcing the issue when the temperatures dropped. For now they sat against the building under the overhang.

Ray leaned his head against the wall and closed his eyes.

"You okay?" Emil asked.

A small smile quirked at Ray's lips.

"I will be. They fed me at least. And had some healer chant over me."

"Did it help?"

"I think so. My head feels clearer."

Ray took his hand and squeezed.

"Thanks for looking out for Stephen."

"Sure."

Emil had more to say, but his brain disconnected from his mouth when Ray rubbed a thumb across his palm like that.

Ray tipped his head to lean it on Emil's shoulder, and Emil turned just enough to press his cheek against Ray's hair.

There. That's a good declaration. Forward, but not too forward.

Ray turned and their lips met. A brief kiss, more of a punctuation to words left unspoken, but the zing of Ray's skin against his rang right through Emil.

Ray smiled. A little chuckle rumbled through his chest. He was feeling it too. Whatever "it" was.

Attraction, definitely, but Emil battled other emotions. Fear was high on the list. Longing too. Anger and guilt rounded out the mix.

After Gabe, he'd thought he would never feel this kind of attraction again—thought he had no right to it. And yet, here he was, feeling like a nervous kid with his first crush.

Emil stared at the bleak faces of the krowa. How could the gods give him this amazing person in a place like this?

Ray was so still, Emil thought he'd fallen asleep, until he said, "We're going to get out of this, right?"

Emil squeezed his hand and felt like another fist gripped his heart.

"We will. I promise."

He'd made other promises—one to Kyra to do everything in his power to bring her the information she needed. And one to himself to never fall in love again and have his heart smashed.

It looked like he'd already broken one of those promises. He just hoped he could keep the others.

EMIL SETTLED INTO LIFE in Pen Five. Faces became familiar. He recognized family units and couples. Women smiled at him. Men frowned until they realized he had no interest in their women. He was becoming accepted, the strange man with the limp and the crutch, the one who never slept, barely ate and couldn't grow a beard. The baby-faced one, he heard one woman call him.

He took pains to be useful. Every morning, he collected the empty buckets and stacked them at the gate. The guard schedule rotated and Teo brought fresh water on Tuesdays and Fridays. Emil never missed a chance to hand the buckets to Teo and catch his eye. Sometimes, the opji would forget himself and thank Emil. Other times, he seemed to make a great effort not to look at him. Either way, Emil knew his continued efforts bothered the guard, and he wanted to know why.

After the guards lugged in the water, Emil helped to distribute buckets, making sure everyone got their fair share. Most thanked him politely with smiles or grunts. Only one man never warmed to Emil. Every time he turned around, Liam was watching him. Liam or his sidekick Neil.

Neil was a short guy with a broad chest and blocky shoulders. He used his bulk to harass the other krowa. He thought it was funny to pretend to lunge at people while they were eating, as if he was going to steal their bowls. His victims inevitably lurched away, spilling the precious gruel. And Neil would laugh.

He took particular pains in tormenting Hamar, a skinny man, old before his time, who had lost most of his mind. Hamar squatted all day beside one of the wood stoves and rocked on his heels. His long gray hair hung in greasy hanks over his face. His mouth, hidden under a thick gray beard, never stopped moving as he babbled, so it looked like a small animal nested between his chin and nose.

Emil didn't know if he never slept, or if he kept up the chatter in his sleep, but Hamar was never silent. He rocked. He stared. And he gabbled.

Ray healed slowly. He tired easily and the meager food rations weren't enough to build up his strength. The gruel the opji provided gave Emil no sustenance at all, but he forced down most of it for appearances. The rest he gave to Ray or Stephen. The kid was always hungry.

Every other night, he hunted rats, draining their blood, then keeping the flesh to be cooked over the fire for the others. The few sips of rat blood wasn't enough to sustain him and he could feel himself growing weaker.

During the day, he spent hours watching the town square, counting bodies. Among the krowa, silent skirmishes flared and were extinguished before the guards caught on.

When Liam wasn't playing sheriff and quelling conflicts, he leaned against the fence with his arms folded across his chest and a scowl on his lip. His eyes often fell on Emil, who would smile and give him a salute. Liam never replied. He just watched.

At night, Ray and Stephen bundled together in their blankets for warmth. On his first night back, Ray had reached out and draped Emil's arm around his shoulder.

"Come on."

It was all the invitation Emil needed. He wrapped his body around Ray and spread his blanket over both of them. There was nothing sexual in the act. Ray was curled around his brother in the same way. But for Emil, it was better than sex. It was comfort. And acceptance.

But as the days and nights wore on and Emil grew hungrier, lying beside a warm human became excruciating. Ray smelled of life. Hot blood flowed through his veins and pulsed at his throat. Emil breathed it in, and with each breath his bloodlust throbbed.

One cold night in December, he could no longer fight the desire. His fangs ached in his gums. He sat up and tucked the scratchy blanket around the brothers.

It had been days since he'd eaten anything but gruel. He needed blood or the scent of Ray would undo him.

A light shone in the yard. Pen Five was never completely dark. The opji probably thought this would keep the krowa from acting out. It didn't stop them from finding comfort of the carnal kind at night. As Emil leaned against the stone wall, he could see at least two piles of blankets shuffling in rhythmic dances.

He ignored them and focused on the shadows along the wall. The scratching of tiny feet alerted him to his prey. Very slowly, while he watched the rat come closer, he separated the blade from his crutch. A quick glance around told him everyone was sleeping or fucking. There would be no one to see.

The rat paused, sat on its hindquarters, and brushed its whiskers with a paw. Emil had a small moment of disquiet as he remembered Raol making the same gesture. Then hunger won over again.

Come on, little blood bag. Just a bit closer.

The rat's head jerked and he turned back the way he'd come. Emil lashed out and pierced it through the neck, pinning it to the dirt with the blade. The rat let out one sharp cry and was silent. Before the blood stopped flowing, Emil drained it.

He licked his lips. One rat wasn't nearly enough to sate him, but it took the edge off so he could think about something other than Ray's throat.

He dropped the body to the side. He'd roast it on the fire for Stephen tomorrow.

While the thorn was out, he nicked a finger and spread blood across the blade. He felt magic shimmer across it as the glamor was renewed. He slipped the thorn back into the wooden shaft of the crutch and set it beside the rat.

A figure rose from the wall and sauntered toward him. Even in the dim light, Emil recognized the bulk of the man. Liam sat beside him, a little too close.

How much had he seen?

Emil decided to pretend all was normal—like he hadn't just drank a rat and blooded a secret blade.

He nodded toward a couple who had just finished their copulation. "You'd think they would know better. That's exactly what the vamps want. A bunch of newborn recruits to the krowa ranks."

"You're new here," Liam said. "You don't get it. After a while, you just don't care anymore."

Emil gave him a noncommittal grunt. The silence grew to awkward proportions but he resisted the urge to fill it with more chatter. Liam clearly had something to say, and he'd wait for it.

Something jabbed Emil in the side. He looked down to see a shank of wood sharpened to a point and ready to stick him in the kidney.

He gaped at Liam whose eyes were black without a hint of emotion. Liam spoke in a rumbling whisper, "Are you a spy?"

"You're opji." It wasn't a question, and Emil didn't answer it. Liam continued in a low voice. "I couldn't figure out the fake limp. But I get it now. You hid a blade in your crutch. It won't help you in here, if the others find out."

"Are you going to tell them?" Emil nodded toward the other sleeping krowa.

Liam jabbed the shank into Emil's side. "I'm not sure yet. I might just kill you and pretend it was an accident."

Panic clawed at Emil's gut. Liam looked like he was born from a pub brawl. Emil was fast, but Liam was bigger and stronger.

He had to make a decision. Did he trust this guy? Since he'd arrived, Emil hadn't seen him fight with anyone. Liam took his meals after everyone else and often gave his rations to old Hamar. He didn't take up with any of the women, and not for lack of female attention. Liam held himself apart. Like a sheriff.

If Emil had to trust someone, it should be the guy with the badge, even if that badge was only implied.

He took a deep breath and spoke fast. "I'm not opji, but I'm not human either. I came here to spy for a group of sympathizers from Montreal. Kyra… my friend…she's gathering an army to come and stop the opji from raiding. Stop them before they turn their attention to Montreal."

"Kyra?"

Out of all that, Liam focused on one name? "Yeah, Kyra Greene. But there are others too. Even some Hub militia who might get involved. They'll be coming soon. I swear."

Emil pressed his head against the wall, not looking at Liam, and waited. If Liam decided to turn him in, his mission was over. A deep rumble came from the man and Emil realized he was laughing.

"She's just bat-shit crazy enough to do it."

Emil turned to gape at him.

"Kyra? You know her?"

Liam nodded and wiped his eyes. "Pretty, braids, creepy sword? Good with animals?"

"That's her!"

"Does she still have a banshee following her?"

"Gita? Well, sort of. I wouldn't say she follows Kyra. More like she nests in the barn."

"Good. That's good. I always wondered what happened to the old bird."

They sat in silence for a while, until Emil asked, "What will you do?"

"Nothing." Liam let his hand holding the shank drop into his lap.

Nothing was better than turning him in, but it wasn't enough. "We have to prepare the others."

"We already are." Liam held up the shank again, and Emil recognized it as the curved edge of one of their gruel bowls, broken clean and sharpened to a point. "We can take only one bowl every few days, so they don't notice them missing."

Emil was impressed. "Does everyone have one of these?"

Liam laughed harshly. "Gods, no. Give this lot knives and they'd be fighting each other in no time. They're buried next to the wall over there." He nodded toward Neil, who slept with his back leaning against the wall.

"Neil's guarding them? Really. But he's such a…" He stopped himself.

"A bully? Yes, he is. But give a bully a purpose and he becomes an ally."

That wasn't Emil's experience. He shook his head. "I'll take your word for it. What are you planning?"

Liam rubbed his chin. His beard was thick and mottled with gray. Emil's face was still clean-shaven. Another thing that set him apart. Another chink in his glamor he hadn't thought about.

"We're not exactly planning," Liam said. "More like preparing for any eventuality. But now…if what you say is true, that an army is really coming…"

"It's true."

Liam smiled, at least his lips spread in a grin, though the light in his eyes was more angry than happy. "Then we have to teach them to fight."

EMIL GAVE UP HIS crutch. It was too difficult to remember to limp, and he left it hidden under their blankets during the day. He thought about burying it like Liam's horde of shank knives, but felt it was better to keep it close at hand.

No one commented on his miraculous recovery when he moved around limp-free.

One Friday morning in January, Emil reluctantly tore himself away from Ray's warmth. The sun wasn't up yet. Ray stirred when he lost the heat from another body. Emil tucked the blanket around him, taking a moment to run his hand along Ray's shoulder. Ray mumbled his name an Emil smiled.

He grabbed their water bucket and the one in the camp next to theirs. That couple—Ben and Shira—were still asleep. He collected more buckets and stacked them by the front gate. Then he waited. Nothing moved. The only sound was Hamar's quiet babble. Emil thought he was saying, "fuck the lights" over and over again, but he couldn't be sure.

He gazed through the chain-link fence at Vioska. The town square was quiet in the pre-dawn hours, but he spotted guards by the Hall of Mages. Night and day, at least half a dozen guards were posted in front of the hall. Emil knew their schedule by heart. He'd spent hours watching the comings and goings at the hall. The guards didn't stop anyone from entering. Even so, they didn't have the bored stance of ceremonial guards. They were there for a reason—a reminder maybe? A warning to those who gathered in the square—or in more secret places—that the would-be king of Vioska made his home inside that hall. And that he was watching.

The answer might be in the explosions he heard from time to time, coming from deep within the hall. At night a beam of light often shot through the domed roof like a laser.

Emil didn't have Kyra's sense of keening, but he knew enough to recognize magic. Something was going on in the hall, some kind of magic experiments, and the king of the opji wanted to protect it.

The sky lightened like a blanket had been pulled off their cage. It would be a while before the sun rose above the rooftops, but there was enough light to see clearly into the streets. And right on time, a horse and cart appeared. It trundled along the alley, coming from the stables. Three opji walked alongside the wagon. Wojaks bounded ahead like rambunctious hounds. As the wagon approached, Emil recognized Teo in the lead.

He moved away from the gate, so he didn't give the trigger-happy guards any excuse to zap him with their prods, and waited. The wagon was turned and backed into the open gate, leaving no chance for krowa to escape. Not that any of them had the energy to try.

Other opji commanders waited outside the pen, but Teo always came inside as the buckets were being unloaded. Emil took this as a sign. He sidled a bit closer and whispered, "Must have fallen below minus ten last night. We could use extra blankets and firewood."

"And yet, you don't look cold," Teo said without looking at him.

Emil let out a gruff laugh. "I have thick blood. But some of the others don't. They suffered."

"It is not my place to care if krowa suffer."

"But you do."

It was a risk, but he really believed that Teo wanted to help the krowa.

Teo's shoulders stiffened. His brown hair was peppered with gray. For an opji that meant he was anywhere from fifty to five-hundred years old. Emil bet he was at the lower end of that bracket. He'd met many long-lived fae in his time. They had a certain apathy that Teo didn't exude. Teo's eyes were deep brown and kind.

Emil had come to Vioska expecting to find monsters. And he had. But what if there were good people hiding among the monsters too? What would happen to them when Kyra's army came crashing down? And did they have any right to being saved if they colluded with the monsters?

He didn't have answers to those questions, and it wasn't his job to find them. But maybe, just maybe, he could persuade this one non-monster to do some good.

"You know this set up you have here is pretty sweet." He leaned against the fence. "Why hunt for food when you can keep a supply on hand. Breed it, in fact. After all isn't that what humans have been doing for thousands of years? Breeding livestock?"

Teo glanced sideways at him without moving. Emil could imagine his incredulity.

"But here's the thing. If you don't care for your livestock properly, they weaken. They die. And that's just a drain of resources, isn't it? Seems like someone at the top isn't all that smart."

Emil knew he'd taken it one step too far with that last comment. Teo straightened his shoulders and turned away.

"You are mistaken, krowa."

The full buckets were unloaded. The empty ones stacked on the wagon bed. Teo barked an order for the guards to move out. He didn't look at Emil again as the gate was slammed and locked.

Emil distributed buckets to sleeping krowa, the ones who were too weak to fetch their water. How many wouldn't wake today? What did they have to wake up for anyway?

Hamar shied away as Emil stepped near. Emil smiled at the mad old goat. Who knew what horrors he'd already endured. Hamar stared at him with wide, terrified eyes, his arms wrapped around his knees as he rocked.

An explosion cut through the calm morning. Confused krowa leapt from their blankets. All eyes locked onto the dome above the Hall of Mages. Smoke billowed from it. The ground shook and krowa clutched at each other or dropped to the dirt. There was no place to take cover. Opji ran from the hall as if it might topple onto their heads. The sky above the dome was lit up like an exploding star.

Behind him, Hamar's babbling turned to shrieking. The blast had been short and the rumble faded away, but the old man had jumped up and pressed his palms to his ears. His eyes were scrunched shut. Then he leaned over, vomited, and passed out in his own mess.

Emil knew a keening overload when he saw one. Hamar wasn't mad. Or at least, he wasn't only mad. His keening sense was off the charts.

The krowa were all awake now and staring at the hall. Smoke drifted from the dome and filled the pen. It was acrid and clung to Emil's throat like ash. People coughed. Some cried.

Hamar woke up and began to rock again. His voice rose in a strange ululation, like a mourner weeping for the dead. Emil half-expected him to start rending his clothes.

"Shut-up!" Neil threw a rock. It glanced off Hamar's temple, drawing a line of blood. The old man didn't even register the assault. He rocked and he wailed.

"I said shut up!" Neil stomped over and kicked Hamar.

"Hey!" Emil shoved him.

The fist came too fast for him to duck. Neil landed the hit and pain lanced through Emil's cheekbone. He staggered back a step, but that was all the satisfaction he'd give the bully. He headbutted him, and felt a sense of satisfaction when his skull connected with Neil's mouth. Neil shook it off, grabbed him by the throat and squeezed.

"Stop it!" Liam pushed between them. Neil let go and stepped back. His eyes flicked toward the square as he wiped his bloody lip on his sleeve. Emil turned too. The fight hadn't attracted the attention of the guards. They were too busy with the bucket brigade that had been set up to bring water into the hall. Something was burning inside.

"Are you insane or just stupid?" Liam snarled.

"Me?" Emil pointed to Neil. "He started it."

"And you're just childish enough to finish it." He turned to Neil. "Go get cleaned up before the guards see you."

Neil made a lunging motion at Emil, and laughed when he flinched, then strode away.

"He's an asshole," Emil said.

"Yes. But if you let him get to you, the guards won't care who started it. They'll toss you both in the wojak pen."

Ray had come looking for him. He took Emil by the hand and led him back to their camp. They had no rags to spare for washing, but he dunked his fingers in their water bucket and rubbed them across Emil's bruised cheek.

"Your skin is so smooth. Like baby skin."

Emil leaned into his touch.

In the weeks they'd been in the pen, Ray had grown a patchy beard. At night, Emil sometimes let his fingers trail over the rough stubble, imagining what it would feel like against more sensitive skin.

"Does it hurt?" Ray's face was inches from his. Their eyes were locked.

"No."

"Liar."

Emil grinned and pain tugged at his cheekbone. It was probably broken, but even in his weakened state, he would heal faster than a human.

Ray carefully washed his face. Emil licked water from his lips, and Ray's eyes caught the motion. He leaned in and kissed him. Emil forgot about the pain and the hunger and all the other discomforts. Instead, he embraced the joy of Ray's beard scuffing his chin and Ray's lips on his. And Ray's scent, like hot blood and wine.

"Oh, geez. Would you guys get a room already?" Stephen popped up between them to take a drink from the water rations.

Emil jerked backward and felt a flush heat his cheeks. Ray just grinned.

"I wish we could, little man. I wish we could." He winked at Emil.

6

The days wore on. The cold set in. Some mornings one of the krowa didn't wake up. The opji guards came in with their prods to pick up the frozen body.

Couples came together at night for warmth and human connection. In the mornings, children stomped on puddles to break the ice and played tag to keep warm. The sound of their laughter seemed a little manic to Emil's ears.

Every morning, he expected to find Hamar dead, but the old man defied the odds. He sat beside his stove, bundled in a blanket and muttering to himself.

Liam started exercising and urged others to join him. At first, Emil thought he was doing it to warm up. He stood in the small clearing under the open sky and moved through a series of Tai Chi exercises. Only a few of the krowa joined in. Their movements were slow and deliberate, just enough to warm the blood, but Emil understood. Tai Chi was more than simple exercise. The postures and flow of movements mimicked hand-to-hand combat. Liam was training his own little army right under the opji's noses.

The rats were getting smarter and Emil was getting weaker. Late one night in January, he left his warm bed to hunt the dark corners of the pen. He caught one rat—the only one he'd found all week. As he bit into its neck, he found Liam watching him. They locked eyes while Emil drank.

Fuck him. He can turn me in or not. I don't care anymore.

Liam said nothing, turning away as Emil licked blood off his lips. The small catch did little to suppress his cravings.

Two nights later he lay under his blanket with Ray pressed against his chest. His nose fit into the little cavern between his ear and his throat. The scent…so hot and alive. It was unbearable.

He sat up, pushed away, and dragged cold air into his lungs. The bloodlust was a hard lump in his throat like a fish bone he could neither swallow nor bring up. He sat against the stone wall. He was already cold, but the stones were colder and they seemed to leach all heat from him. His gaze caught on the light filtering up through the dome of the Hall of Mages. Ichovidar was working late tonight. Was he creating some new weapon that would finally bring the humans and fae of Montreal to heel?

Gods, he needed to get inside that building, but he didn't know how, short of giving up his charade and telling the opji what he really was. Who he really was.

No. He wasn't ready for that. Part of his fear was being forced to take the zycha rite, and how that would change him. But he also worried about being taken away from Ray and Stephen. How would he protect them then?

He watched the magic rise on colorful waves from the hall until the cold was too much to bear. Then he slipped back under his blankets and tried to still his shivering against Ray's back. The bloodlust returned, quick and sharp like a knife wound, and the shivering turned into trembling.

Ray pressed against him. "I know what you want. Why don't you just do it?" He arched his neck, exposing a thick vein. "Go on." He whispered. "Take some. You need it."

Emil hissed and pedaled backward, pushing Ray away. Stephen, lying on the other side, stirred in his sleep. Ray tucked the blanket around him and turned his back to his brother.

"How long have you known?" Emil asked.

"Since the first time you went hunting for rats." Ray took Emil's fingers and pressed them against the pulse throbbing at his wrist.

"You can't live on rats. And I'm not afraid of you." He lifted his chin defiantly.

Gods, he was beautiful. Even the harshness of fatigue and hunger didn't diminish the light inside him.

"You should be," Emil whispered. Thirst was a hard, hot knot in his chest.

"Well, I'm not. You won't hurt me."

"Yes! Yes, I will. You're too weak. I could take too much."

"You won't." He wrapped warm hands around Emil's wrists and tugged him forward. Emil resisted.

"No, no, no." He sounded like Hamar, babbling into the darkness.

Ray held out his arms. "Come on. At least get warm."

Emil let himself be drawn in.

Just to get warm. Nothing more.

He turned his back so Ray spooned him from behind, and that way all he could smell was the piss and shit from the pen's waste buckets.

Eventually, the shivering died down.

Ray tightened his arms around Emil. His breath was hot in his ear as he whispered, "You know I won't last 'til spring. In the end, you will take what you need. And live. Promise me. You'll live so you can take care of Stephen."

Emil had no answer to that.

Shouting from across the square made him set aside any further argument. He sat up.

The night lit up in yellow and red. At first he thought the Hall of Mages was on fire again, but the shouting came from the other direction, toward the edge of town.

Kyra! It had to be Kyra and Mason and Hub, finally come to free them!

Hope melted the numbness around his mind. And brought clarity.

It was too early for Kyra to attack. He'd lost track of the days while in captivity. One water bucket looked much like another. But the cold and the long nights told him it was still January. Kyra wouldn't leave Montreal for weeks yet.

But something was happening in Vioska.

He joined the other krowa at the chain-link fence. Fingers grasped the cold wire as faces pressed against it for a better look. Screams echoed through the empty square. Across the way, the newly turned wojaks were agitated in their pen. They hollered like monkeys and slammed their wasted bodies against the fences.

Smoke and shouts filled the air. The flickering light of flames appeared over rooftops to the east. Emil tried to remember from his short trip through the square what lay down that lane.

"It's another krowa pen," Liam said, joining him at the fence. "Sounds like they're rioting."

They listened until the screams faded, leaving the night full of smoke. And ominous silence.

"Get ready!" Liam shot the command at the krowa still pressed against the fence. He pointed to Ray and another couple. "Keep the kids to the back. Protect them if you can."

Emil grabbed his arm. "What's going on?"

In the dark, Liam's face was unreadable. "The guards will come. They'll want to be sure we don't get ideas from them." He nodded toward the flames still rising above the unseen krowa pen. "And they'll want revenge."

From across the square, shadows began to converge. The opji were coming.

"Don't fight them!" Liam urged as the krowa ran from the fence to huddle in groups by the far wall, as if the cold stones offered protection. But Emil knew the truth: there was no protection against what was coming.

He ran to their camp. His cold fingers grappled with the pile of bedding as he uncovered his crutch. Hefting it in his hands he felt stronger than he had in weeks.

Liam pointed at him. "Don't use that. They'll kill you."

Emil grinned and spun the crutch in his grip to hold it like a spear. The cushioned top had come unraveled from the head and a bit of brass shone through.

Liam shook his head and went to stand by the gate to greet the incoming force.

He's offering himself as the sacrificial lamb.

Seconds later, Emil was proven right. The opji guards came through the door with cattle prods blazing. They hit Liam in the chest first, giving him no chance to retaliate. He went down convulsing.

But Liam's sacrifice did nothing to quell the raging guards. They moved through the crowded pen, threatening some of the cowering krowa, jabbing others just for good measure. No one resisted. No one fought back. Bodies fell, wracked by seizures.

Emil stood in front of the children with Ray by his side. The kids' parents circled them as if their arms could hold off the violence.

Hamar's babbling reached an ear-piercing crescendo, and then he too fell under the prod. The lead guard seemed to take pleasure in his job and he zapped the unconscious Hamar again and again. Just for shits and giggles.

Then he stood in front of Emil. And Ray. And the kids.

"Move." The opji's thick accent made it sound like a grunt.

Emil didn't move.

The prod lashed out. He deflected it with the crutch. The opji went high. Emil parried. A low cut. A high slash. Faster. The jabs kept coming and Emil kept blocking. Left shoulder. Block. Knees. Block. He wanted to unleash the thorn's blade but the opji gave him no chance. All he could do was parry and push back and parry again. Lady Lughwaite's fencing lessons finally proved their worth.

The prod slammed into the shaft of the crutch, inches from his nose. He smelled the zing of galvanic magic sizzling on its tip. Holding the crutch with two hands, he pushed.

Emil hadn't eaten anything but rat for weeks. The opji was strong, full of life-giving blood.

He grinned. His fangs glowed unnaturally white in the dim light.

Ray screamed. A second guard had slipped around to jab him. Ray fell, foaming at the mouth as volts of energy surged through him.

Emil's world went black. With rage. He lashed out, thrusting the opji backward, swung wide, not caring that he left himself exposed and brought the brass head down on the opji's skull.

And as the prod jabbed him and the seizures took him, he grinned, knowing he'd got in one good hit.

C H A P T E R

7

He woke to the sound of his own heart beating loudly in his ears. Lying on the damp ground, he reached for his crutch. His fingers found only dirt. He sat up, hands searching the ground around him.

"They took it." Ray sat against the fence. A cut oozed blood above his right eye. His beard didn't quite mask the bruise blossoming across his cheek. Stephen crouched beside his brother, his eyes wide and, for once, out of words.

Emil did a quick internal check. Whatever beating the opji had inflicted on him, the wounds were already healed.

"You look different," Ray said. His words were slightly garbled because the whole right side of his face was swollen. The guards hadn't just zapped him. They'd beaten him. Probably in retaliation for Emil's actions.

"Oh yeah? You look like shit." Emil kept his tone light, like he wasn't panicking. Ray looked bad. Really bad. He could barely hold his head off the fence.

Ray smiled, and his lip started to bleed again. Stephen let out a little mewl of dismay and crawled into Ray's lap. Ray patted him, but his eyes rested on Emil.

"No really, you look different. More alive, somehow."

Emil tried to brush the comment aside. "I just like a good fight."

Ray shook his head, but he was still smiling. Emil wished he could muster even a fraction of Ray's good humor.

He rose and walked toward the fence to look out at Vioska. The Thorn of Vidar was somewhere in town. How far? Too far to keep up his glamor?

But he already knew the answer to that question. The thorn was gone. The glamor was gone. Ray's eyes following him proved it. His mundane senses might not understand what he was seeing, but his instincts did. Others watched him curiously, sensing the change, but not knowing exactly what that change was.

Only Hamar wasn't fooled.

The opji had beaten him unconscious, but when he woke, the first thing he did was point to Emil and scream, "Vampire!" Then he sunk to a crouch and started digging in the dirt, babbling and drooling. The other krowa took this as a sign that all was normal again.

But Emil knew it was only a matter of time before the opji realized he wasn't human.

He crouched beside Ray, who sat with his eyes closed and head resting against the wall. At first, Emil thought he was unconscious, but when he touched his shoulder, Ray opened one swollen eye.

Emil used the last of their water to wash Ray's face, taking pains to be gentle around his split lip and bruises.

"Listen," he whispered urgently. "They'll be coming for me soon."

"Coming…" Ray could barely speak and Emil saw that he was having trouble focusing.

"Yes. They'll take me from the pen." He swallowed down his panic. The opji might just kill him. "If they do, I don't want you to fight. You have to get better."

"Don't…don't go." Ray's weak fingers clutched at Emil's arm.

Emil leaned in and tucked his nose into the crook of Ray's neck, breathing in his scent and committing it to memory.

"I have to. I'm sorry." He pulled away and cupped the side of Ray's face. "You have to stay strong. For Stephen. For me." His voice hitched and he sucked in a breath. "There's an army coming. Humans and fae. I swear it. My friend, Kyra, sent me here to spy on the opji. If I can, I'll go to her. But I swear, I'll be back to free you."

Tears leaked down Ray's battered face.

"Go. Don't come back."

Emil shook his head. "I *am* coming back." He placed a gentle kiss on Ray's swollen lips, then left him to sleep.

Stephen sat nearby, looking scared.

"You'll watch over him until he's better?" Emil asked.

Stephen nodded and hugged his knees.

"Is it true what you said? You'll come back with an army."

"It's true, but you must keep that to yourself. Don't even tell Freddie, okay?"

Stephen nodded. Emil didn't trust him to keep the secret, but it didn't matter. If the opji heard him, they'd never believe a krowa kid.

Emil collected empty water buckets. Krowa watched with guarded expressions, but they always did.

Liam approached him at the gate as Emil stacked empty buckets.

"You should stay out of their way today." Liam's right eye was purple and he spoke with the lisp of a swollen tongue. He gripped Emil's arm. "I heard what you did, saving the kids. It was…good." He stumbled over the word as if the concept of goodness was hard for him to admit. "Best to let them forget about you for a few days."

Emil thought he was probably right, but the guards were already pushing the cart toward the gate. It swung open as he backed away, right into Neil. The man's hands gripped Emil's elbows, locking him in place.

"If they want a scapegoat, I'm giving them you."

"Don't be so sure," Emil said. "You smell like a goat. They might get confused."

Neil growled into his ear, and kicked out the back of his leg. Emil fell to one knee.

"Stop!" Liam hissed and jerked Neil away. "Don't give them more reason to fight!"

The bully smiled and shrugged. He reached a hand out to help Emil up. Emil spat in the dirt and ignored the gesture. He stood, ready to take Liam's suggestion and fade into the background.

But it was too late.

The first opji guard through the gate stared at him. He held his cattle prod in one hand, but it was lowered as he gaped at Emil.

Was he that obvious? Did every opji suddenly recognize him for what he was?

Yes, and yes.

The guard started shouting. Emil understood only one word in five. Mage. Zycha. Opji.

The cart full of water was pushed back. The gate slammed shut. Groans went up from the krowa waiting for water rations.

Emil turned to flee into the crowd but Liam caught him.

"What did you do?"

"Nothing! I swear!"

The opji were already coming back.

"Let them have him," Neil snarled, but they all knew there was no "letting." The opji came. They took what they wanted.

A few minutes later, the gate opened again. Four opji stood there with Teo in the lead. He was unarmed, but the opji behind him wielded prods, and behind them a row of wojaks paced, ready for any blood bag tossed their way.

Teo stared at Emil. His thin brows were pressed down as he tried to work out what his senses were telling him. Then his eyes widened.

"No!"

Emil stepped forward. He reached for Teo's arm but the opji behind him raised their prods and he froze.

He heard Ray calling his name from the back of the pen.

Better to get this over with before the guards took notice of Ray and Stephen.

Emil bowed his head and held out his hands in surrender.

Teo took his arm. As he turned Emil toward the gate, he whispered, "I'm sorry. I have no choice."

He didn't speak again as he escorted Emil through the empty square and up the steps of the Hall of Mages. The wojaks left them at the doors of the hall—a detail Emil thought was interesting—but two of the guards standing outside joined their little parade. They marched him through the doors and into a round atrium. Glass covered candles hung from sconces around the room. The light was barely enough to reach the high ceiling.

Emil paused to gape at the ornate carvings that were everywhere he looked. Frescoes etched along the curved walls depicted hunting scenes. Opji chasing humans, deer and bear. The crown moldings were leafless vines with prominent thorns, like fangs that seemed to bite into the walls and ceiling. The ceiling itself was painted deep blue with flecks of gold leaf that glittered in the candlelight.

A guard shoved him roughly from behind and Emil stumbled. Booted feet clopped on the stone floor as they marched him through the atrium and down a long hallway. They turned right and continued. The halls were lit by more candles that never quite filled the shadows lurking in the corners. More turns, left and then right again, up stairways and down, until Emil lost his sense of place. They could have been in the basement or a tower for all he knew.

Finally, Teo stopped in front of a single oak door, again carved with elaborately snarling predators—wolves, bears, lions. He didn't knock, but only waited with his head bowed until a deep voice commanded him from within. He opened the door and moved aside, letting Emil precede him.

Emil stepped into a large office. A desk filled most of the space on the right. To the left, Ichovidar sat on a couch before a hearth with a low-burning fire.

He smiled and spoke in heavily accented English. "Welcome home, Janzek."

The name shivered across Emil's mind like it was laced in magic. It was both familiar and strange. He wished he had Kyra's ability to block magic attacks because he was standing before the most powerful mage in Vioska, and he was dirty, tired, and weak. Vulnerable. But even in his weakened state, he could feel Ichovidar's magic weaving around him like an invisible snare. He pulled his gaze away and surveyed the room, committing details to memory. This was his chance to get real information.

The room was spare, almost utilitarian. The intricate carvings stopped at the door and the office walls were bare plaster. The only decorations were the wrought iron wall sconces shaped like thorns again, and the fieldstone hearth. A bookshelf rose behind the desk, filled with books, scrolls and paraphernalia of the dark arts—black candles, mortars, statuettes carved from obsidian. It was the space of a mage, not his workroom, but his retreat, a place he could go to think and read undisturbed.

Emil's eyes trailed back to Ichovidar, perched in the middle of the couch. Even sitting, he could tell the mage-king was tall. And maybe he'd once been strong, but he seemed shrunken. His features were blocky with high cheekbones and a square jaw, but skin hung from his jowls unpleasantly like he'd recently lost a lot of weight too quickly. The white blond hair that marked his lineage was thinning and hung in greasy strands past his shoulders.

He's worn himself out in his relentless pursuit of…whatever he's doing here. Emil took some small satisfaction from that, but despite this disheveled appearance, Ichovidar seemed to emanate power as if he sat inside a cocoon of magic.

His hands moved incessantly, caressing the artifact in his lap.

It was the Thorn of Vidar. The crutch was gone and only the knife remained in its wooden sheath topped by the brass eagle.

"Thank you for this. It is a treasure that belongs in Vioska. It will have a place of honor in our house and be a symbol of our victory. Tell me, how did you activate its glamor?"

"I am—" Emil's voice came out in a squeak. He cleared his throat and tried again. "I am a great mage…" He trailed off as Ichovidar shook with silent laughter.

"You?" He used the thorn to point at Emil. His laughter died away. "You are nothing. You come here, under false pretenses to what? To spy? You are not a *mago*." He sneered the opji word. "You are a fraud. But you are used to that, aren't you? The opji living as a human all his life. A fraud. The human-lover trying to be the opji. Fraud again." He unsheathed the blade hidden inside the thorn and ran its edge along the back of his hand. His eyes went from the blade to Emil and he said, "You know, no matter what they told you, I'm not your father."

Emil didn't know who "they" were, but the idea that Ichovidar could be his father had never occurred to him.

Darkness seethed on the periphery of his vision.

It's hunger. Just hunger.

He closed his mind to the idea that magic was suffocating him.

Ichovidar's voice lashed out like a silent whip. "She was a slut, your mother. She lay with half the council, always looking for the one who would bring her power and prestige."

Ichovidar had a way of bowing his head and looking up at the same time. It accentuated his dark eyes, made him seem almost coy. "She was a good fuck though." He slammed the knife back into the sheath and rose.

Sitting on the couch, Ichovidar had been formidable. Standing, he loomed over Emil. The bulk of his shoulders seemed to fill the small space. His hand reached forward and Emil could do nothing but watch it come for him.

"You are an abomination." A finger jabbed him in the chest with each word. Emil toppled backward, and he was shocked by his own frailty. Teo caught him, and shoved him forward.

Ichovidar turned and walked over to the bookshelf, placing the thorn among the scrolls.

"I heard there was an opji living among the fae, but I didn't dare to hope that one could live in such a weakened state for so long." He turned and placed his hands flat on the desk. He cocked his head as if considering prey. "You are weak. But we will fix you. You will be a great asset. The fae and the humans trust you. We can use that."

Emil found his voice. "I will never betray my family."

"Your family?" Ichovidar laughed. "They will never know what it is like to crave blood, to reap the benefits of hot, liquid iron in your veins. They can never be your family. We are."

Emil was shaking with rage and fear or the bastard child of both—the desire to kill. His heart thudded and his hands clenched at his side. Some part of his mind understood that Ichovidar was forcing this reaction. Fingers of magic tugged at him, pushed at him, clawed into his mind. But he didn't care. All he wanted to do was bite that alabaster neck and rip out his throat.

He lurched toward the desk, his feet propelled by emotions he couldn't control.

Teo and another guard restrained him. He lashed out, straining against their grip.

Ichovidar smiled. "Good. You have fight in you. And rage. Both will work in your favor when you take the *zycha*. And then your family in Montreal will be nothing more than a meal that got away. Take him."

Ichovidar flicked his hand and the guards dragged him away.

CHAPTER

9

They tossed him in a bare cell. Teo said quietly, "Don't fight them," then closed the heavy metal door. A dead bolt clanged into place, leaving an echo that reverberated through Emil's aching head.

Ichovidar had definitely been weaving magic in that room, but for what purpose? To control him? To wring the truth from him? Or just because he could?

Emil collapsed and hugged the cold stone floor. As the magic left him, he felt less woozy but more scared.

He had miscalculated. Badly. Ichovidar wasn't just some vampire king. He was a powerful mage. And possibly his father. How had he ever believed he could stand up to him?

A sob broke from his throat and he pounded a fist on the floor. He was a vampire, for god's sake. He wasn't afraid of pain or even dying. But this…this was a battle for his soul.

The zycha would change him. It would slow his heart and calm his bloodlust, yes. But it would also link him intimately and forever with the opji. And more than that. Ichovidar intimated what Emil already suspected—the zycha would alter his personality. Would it channel the bloodlust into another emotion—rage, hate or conceit? Was that the driving force behind the opji's genocidal tendencies?

He had no answers, but only the conviction that he had to escape and warn Kyra. And he had to do it before they forced that dark rite on him.

A LITTLE LIGHT FILTERED through the barred window on the door. The cell's only furniture was a bucket of water. In the first hours of his captivity, Emil paced. Six steps in length and seven in width.

Six. Seven. Six. Seven.

The shuffle of his footsteps became a mantra. He tried to form thoughts, make plans for escape, but his mind was blank.

Six. Seven. Six. Seven.

The deadbolt clanged and the cell door swung open. Emil expected guards or maybe Teo, but a stranger stood in the doorway.

Small and wiry, he wore his hair long and loose around his shoulders in the same fashion as Ichovidar's, though this man's hair was black. Instead of the usual dark woolen uniform, he wore a midnight blue robe.

A mage.

Emil rushed him. The mage stepped out of the way. Emil lurched into the hallway and right onto the spear of a guard. The metal tip pierced his shoulder.

He hissed. Unfazed, the guard jerked the spear, shoving Emil back into the cell. He twisted the weapon and pulled it free, leaving a ragged hole in Emil's shirt and flesh. The wound leaked blood and was slow to heal. He was too weak.

"Calm yourself, Janzek. No one here will hurt you."

Emil balled his fists. "Stop calling me that!" His words were slurred. He was so very tired.

The mage cocked his head. "But why not? It is your name. I was there at your birth when your mother gave it to you." The mage touched a finger to the blood on his shoulder and licked it. "You taste like her. Full of busy energy. Buzz, buzz, buzz. A busy little bee just like Tereza." He tapped his finger and thumb together and pretended they could fly.

Who the hells was this idiot?

Emil swung his fist. The mage was faster and ducked out of the way. The follow through of his punch brought Emil to one knee. He stayed there, panting, while he thought of his next move.

The mage smiled down on him, completely unperturbed by his outburst.

"My name is Sylwan. I am here to help you." He laid a hand on Emil's head. "I understand that this must be frightening. I promise to explain everything as it happens, since you haven't enjoyed the formal catechism for the zycha." His fingers kneaded Emil's scalp. It was soothing and mesmerizing. The mage's voice droned on. "I can see that you have been badly indoctrinated, taught to fear what you don't understand. Taught to despise your own heritage. That must be very lonely. We will fix that. But first we must make you strong or you won't survive the zycha."

He snapped his fingers as he left the cell. The door wasn't locked. Emil lifted his head, but any hope of escaping was dashed when a guard appeared gripping a human woman roughly by the elbow. He jerked her arm upward and she let out a shrill cry, then he shoved her into the cell and closed the door. The lock engaged.

The woman had fallen to the floor. She looked up and her face was only inches from his. Blond hair fell over her eyes, messed from the rough handling, but it had been recently brushed and she was clean for a krowa. She took one look at Emil and scuttled away like a crab to press herself into the corner.

Emil sighed and scooted to the other side of the room.

They wanted him to feed. He wouldn't. But of course, she didn't know that.

Emil sat with his knees drawn up to his chin. The room was too dark. He could barely make out the woman's outline, but he could hear her. She sniffled and panted. Starving as he was, Emil's senses were heightened. He could smell her moist breath, hear the faint pulse of her blood.

"I'm not going to hurt you," he said into the darkness, but instead of reassuring her, the woman began to sob. Fear had overloaded her senses.

Emil locked his arms around his knees and steeled himself against the hunger.

Hours later, he was a hair away from giving in to the bloodlust, if only to shut up the blubbering krowa. His fingers were raw from clawing at the stone floor.

Just as he shoved upward, ready to lunge, the cell door opened. A guard grabbed the woman and hauled her out. A second guard replaced his empty water bucket with a fresh one.

Emil crawled across the floor. His legs trembled with pins and needles. His fingers fumbled on the lip of the bucket, and he spilled it over his face as he drank. When he'd had his fill, he lay on the floor, physically wasted, emotionally wrung out. And, he realized with growing concern, inebriated.

They'd drugged the water.

Sylwan returned. He stood over Emil and *tsked* like he was disappointed in an unruly student.

A chair was brought in. Two guards hauled him up and dumped him onto it. He teetered sideways and nearly hit the floor before they caught him. His head lolled back.

"I'm sorry for this." Sylwan tapped the water bucket with his foot. Emil could see the notes of his melodious voice floating in the air. He giggled.

Sylwan frowned. "I hoped you would accept our gift of blood, but I can see your indoctrination runs too deeply." He leaned in so that his whole face filled Emil's vision. "I need you to be healthy. You want to be healthy, yes?"

Emil worked up enough saliva to spit. The gob rose a few inches in the air and splatted him on the nose. He giggled again.

"Hold him." Sylwan's voice grew stern.

Uh-oh. I'm in trouble now.

"Not in trouble, Janzek. We're going to help you."

Emil's head lolled to the side. He hadn't realized he'd spoken aloud.

His jaws were pried apart and a plastic tube shoved into his mouth. He gagged, but then the drugs really kicked in and he sagged like a limp noodle. All thought flitted away.

Hot, thick blood pulsed into his throat.

And he drank.

They returned every day to force feed him. He refused to drink the drugged water, so the guards held him down while Sylwan injected him.

Emil gave silent prayers for the krowa who gave up their blood for him.

Each time the drug wore off, he woke feeling stronger and sharper than he had in years. Human blood had never been part of his diet. That was the rule Queen Leighna had forced on him in exchange for the privilege of living in Montreal. He'd survived on pig's blood. Now, with the magic-rich human blood coursing through him, he understood what he'd been missing. He could feel every hair on his body tingle with sensitivity, like the feelers on a spider sensing vibrations in its web.

On the fourth day, instead of bringing a chair and shackles, the guards lugged in a washtub. They returned with buckets of hot water to fill it. An opji woman arrived, carrying a basket of soaps and brushes along with fresh towels. She didn't speak English, but gestured for him to strip and get in the tub.

Emil shot a glance at the guard who stood by the closed door. He sighed. There would be no getting out of this. They would drug him if he didn't comply, and in truth, he longed for a bath.

The attendant wrinkled her nose when he handed over his filthy shirt and pants. He sank into the tepid water with a groan and reached for the basket of soap. The woman swatted his hand away, then scooped water with a cup and poured it over his head. When she lathered his hair and began massaging his scalp with her nails, Emil's bones turned to rubber. He let her scrub him, rinse him and dress him in a fresh white smock as if he were a small child.

When she was done, Sylwan appeared.

"Ah, so there *is* a handsome man under all that dirt." He looked pleased. The bath attendant nodded and left with her baskets.

"How are you feeling?" Sylwan asked.

Emil crossed his arms and refused to answer. He would give the mage nothing. Sylwan pinched his cheek. "There's some color to your flesh at least." He clapped his hands. "Yes, I believe you're ready."

The guards appeared again, one on each side to manhandle Emil out the door and down the long corridor. After only a couple of turns and one staircase, Sylwan led them into a small hall. It had the feel of a church with a dais at the far end and a large open space before it, where Emil could imagine spectators. Today—tonight? Emil had no idea of the time—the room was empty.

On the dais was a podium where one might give a sermon. A font stood beside that, full of some dark liquid. Most of the dais was taken up by a large stone bed with censers on tall rods at the four corners. The entire wall behind the altar was made of drawers—small, square and numbered like an apothecary.

The guards shoved him onto the stone bed and shackled his wrists and ankles.

"Don't worry," Sylwan said. "The shackles are standard procedure. The zycha is usually done on young boys and girls. It can be painful. I'm sure you won't find it too uncomfortable, but…" He let out a laugh. "I hear your thoughts as clearly as if spoken aloud." He leaned in closer. "There is no escape. Guards wait in the hall, and at every passage. They have been alerted to your unusual situation. So, I know you won't be foolish and try to escape." He turned to a small table laid out with surgical-looking instruments. When he turned around again, he held a tube with a rubber bulb on the end like a short turkey baster. "Still, I need you calm." He squeezed the bulb and a puff of moist air misted over Emil's face.

He tried not to breathe it in, but within seconds, he felt himself melting and floating at the same time. Unlike the drugs they'd pumped into him in his cell, this one seemed to heighten his awareness. The plaster on the ceiling became a fascinating map of cracks and stains. He could smell the wall of drawers that exuded an earthy and metallic scent. Sylwan seemed to have a nimbus of light around him as he puttered with his tools and narrated what he was doing.

"Of course all opji children know about the zycha and welcome it as a time of celebration. But I understand that you know nothing of the sacred rite. I will explain it, so you will see there is nothing to fear."

Emil moved his lips to tell the mage to go fuck himself, but his tongue felt like pudding in his mouth, and the sound he made was little more than a moan. Sylwan chose a knife from his instruments and slit Emil's tunic from the neck all the way down. He spread the cloth wide, leaving Emil naked and exposed.

"The zycha is a gift, given to the opji by God on the day He made man. You see we were here first. Opji means, *first blood*. And that's how God made us, not in his image. In his blood."

It's always about the blood, Emil tried to say, but again his words were little more than a groan.

Sylwan laid out a mortar and pestle beside a fresh cloth.

"And that's what runs in our veins. We hunger for God's blood. But, alas, we can never taste it again. So we settle for human blood."

Who says "alas?" What a putz.

"The need for more and more blood to fill this void threatened to consume us, and so the ancient opji were given another gift—the knowledge to dull the bloodlust. It has other benefits, of course. Your lifespan will be extended by hundreds of years. Your strength will double. You'll heal even faster, and the greatest gift of all—you will be opji. A true opji. The zycha is more than a ceremony, just as being opji is more than a heritage or a way of life. The zycha will alter your perceptions at a cellular level. You will finally be free to understand the true superiority of God's first children."

And that was exactly what Emil feared. The zycha wouldn't just quell his bloodlust. It would mind-fuck him in ways he would never recover from.

He thrashed against the restraints. The chains jangled but held.

Sylwan smiled and didn't bother to reproach him. He lit the censers at the four corners and cloying smoke filled the air.

Emil laid his head back and gave up the fight against his bonds. The room spun.

Sylwan turned to the wall of drawers, searched for a particular number and opened it.

"To be honest, I never thought I would open this drawer again." He pulled out a red silk pouch, opened the drawstrings and dumped several clumps of blackened…something into his hand. He held it out for Emil to see. "This is yours. Your first meal and pillow. The placenta that nourished and comforted you in your mother's womb. I preserved it myself and put it away only weeks after you were born, before your mother's betrayal." He sighed like the wound was still fresh, then dumped the black lumps into the mortar and started to grind.

Emil's muscles stopped responding. He could no longer hold up his head to watch, and it dropped to the stone table with a thud. His brain urged arms and legs to pull at the shackles, but his limbs were puddles of mush. Sweat beaded on his forehead and dripped into his eyes.

Sylwan finished his preparations. From the corner of his eye, Emil watched him sprinkle a pinch of ground placenta into each brazier. The fires sparked and burned with a new sweet scent. He added the rest of the powder to a new bowl and stirred. When he lifted the spoon to test the consistency, it dripped with red viscous fluid.

More blood. Emil had the hysterical urge to giggle.

Sylwan drenched a small white cloth in the mixture, squeezed it out and laid it aside. Then he leaned over Emil and smiled, showing him his red stained hands.

"A little fresh paint for you."

He dipped his fingers in the bowl and smeared blood across Emil's forehead.

Emil longed to turn away, but could only stare straight into Sylwan's eyes.

The mage anointed him—down his cheeks, across his heart and his genitals, dipping his fingers for fresh blood each time.

Sylwan lifted Emil's head.

"Here now. Don't fight me."

A metallic tang hit his tongue as Sylwan drizzled blood into his mouth. His lungs contracted and he coughed, spraying Sylwan with speckles of blood. The mage frowned and wiped his face on his sleeve. His friendly expression turned dark. He dipped a knife into the blood and held it in front of Emil's nose. The blade was long and thin, with a wickedly sharp point. Blood coated the first two inches of blade.

"This will hurt."

Sylwan sliced Emil's cheek, dipped the blade again and cut the other one. Then Emil lost sight of him, but he felt each prick of the blade, tiny jabs down his chest, arms and legs. The mage no longer spoke. He chanted in a deep resonating voice. The sound mixed with the smoke from the braziers and seemed to swirl around him, building in power like the air before a thunderstorm.

Sylwan's voice rose to a crescendo and he shouted, "Kra!" His arms rose and he shouted again. Emil recognized a calling.

"Kra!" Magic coalesced in the echo of that word. It hung in the air like a live thing.

"Kra!" Sylwan's voice was full of command and he plunged the knife into Emil's heart.

Emil seized. His breath shuddered to a stop. Magic slammed into him like a bolt of lightning. He jerked. His back arched. The shackles dug into his wrists. Then he thumped back onto the table.

His heart slowed. His lungs ceased their labor. The edges of his vision turned dark and fuzzy.

Sylwan laid the blood-soaked cloth over his face. Emil felt the weight of a hand across his eyes.

"Sleep, Janzek of the Opji."

And Emil died.

CHAPTER

10

Emil woke with the feel of a hand on his chest. He sat bolt upright.

"Easy, Janzek." Sylwan pushed him gently back onto the pillow. "You must go easy for the first hours. Let your body get used to its new, how do you say it…configuration."

"I thought…" Emil's voice grated. He cleared his throat and tried again. "I thought I was dead."

"You were, but only so you could be reborn. How do you feel?"

Emil fisted his hands and flexed his feet.

"I feel…strong."

"Good, good." Sylwan peered into his eyes. "You will make a strong soldier, yes? We need soldiers. No more talk of running away, yes?" His brows pressed low over his eyes. Emil could see this question was very important.

"No running."

Sylwan nodded as if he'd expected as much. He patted Emil on the shoulder and rose. "Rest for the day, then tomorrow you start to train. You are opji now! Welcome home."

He left and Emil sat up in the bed. Other than the silence in his chest, he seemed intact. His heart beat once—a sound like a single strike of a jackhammer—then went silent again. He waited a full minute before it beat again. That would take some getting used to.

He turned his head toward the only window in the room and the world kaleidoscoped. He gripped the edge of the bed until the wooziness passed and tasted blood. He'd bitten his tongue. The metallic flavor zinged through him.

Every one of his senses was heightened. The walls of the small room were bland white, but the plaster seemed to throb with veins and bumps. He ran a hand over it, and was thrilled by the sensation under his fingers. From outside he heard doors banging and low conversations.

He examined his surroundings. The room was small, with only a cot, a chest and a washstand. A dark uniform was laid out on the chest. The ceiling sloped and a recessed window filled the room with weak afternoon light. He rose and looked outside. He was on the second floor, across the street from a barracks. He assumed he was in a similar building.

Opji soldiers came and went. Some loitered in the street. Emil's newly acute eyesight picked out their lips moving and even through the closed window he could just make out the sounds of their conversations. No wonder the opji were a silent broody lot, if everyone around you could hear even the most intimate conversations.

His gaze was drawn beyond the rooftops, to the impressive dome of the Hall of Mages. He was at least a mile from the center of town, and the distance was filled with buildings and twisted lane ways. He hadn't realized Vioska was so big.

And surrounding the entire town was a red haze like a domed lid on a dinner platter. His heightened opji senses now let him see the ward.

Kyra always said that everyone has at least a touch of the keening. Mundanes call it intuition. It was also a skill that could be honed, though Emil had never bothered with it. Now he wished he had. Maybe then he could make sense of what he was seeing. The ward was transparent, but sparks of energy writhed across it, like tiny worms squirming across its surface.

Wow. He needed to get this information to Kyra. Invading Vioska would be more than a manned onslaught. She would need magical interference to even get close enough to fight the opji.

He sat on the bed and did his final examination, turning his eye inward.

Sylwan had assumed—as Emil had—that the zycha rite would fundamentally change him. It would imbue him with the zealotry that fueled all opji. Emil searched his feelings for a long time. Did he detect a burning need to slaughter innocent humans? No. He thought of Kyra and Mason. And Gita. And Ray and Stephen. He belonged to them, not the opji.

It occurred to him that no one who had been raised outside opji influence had ever taken the zycha.

They'd just assumed.

They believed it would solidify the very opji-ness inside him. It did no such thing. His thoughts tracked that idea to its inevitable conclusion.

If the rite didn't make him fundamentally opji, then maybe…just maybe, there were others in Vioska who felt the same as him. Maybe there were others who sympathized with the krowa.

Emil dressed in the black woolen uniform that was laid out for him and went looking for Teo.

THE LOWER LEVEL OF the barracks contained a communal bath and a large hall filled with tables and benches, like a mess hall except there was no kitchen, only a counter with jugs of water.

Of course, opji wouldn't need kitchens.

Emil poured water into a mug just for something to do and sat at one of the long tables. A few other soldiers lounged in the hall. Eyes had followed him when he first entered, but by the time he sat, they'd turned away. Emil straddled a bench and sipped his water, wondering what he should do next. Would someone come in and give him orders? Was he free to explore Vioska?

A dozen doors lined the long wall of the hall. Most were ajar but three were closed. Emil had decided to start his explorations there, when one of the doors opened. A soldier came out, dragging a man behind him. He was human and young and had a used look—hair messed, eyes glassy, lethargic gait. The soldier hauled him to a room at the end of the hall and handed him off to a clerk, who made a note in a ledger.

As the soldier left, the clerk shoved the krowa, and he sprawled into the darkness beyond Emil's sight.

Emil's stomach turned sour.

That was a feeder krowa. This *was* a mess hall, but the only food available was human blood. He sat for another half hour watching opji come in, sign out human blood bags and retire to the feeding chambers.

A new chill ran through him. He hadn't realized feeding was monitored. In truth, he hadn't thought past getting inside Vioska. How would he avoid drinking human blood if they kept a tally of feedings like rations?

Another soldier entered the hall. He met Emil's eye and turned right back around.

Teo.

Emil jumped up and joined him as he emerged into the street.

Teo sped up but Emil matched his pace. When they turned a corner away from the barracks, Teo finally slowed, but he would not look at Emil.

"What do you want?"

"I just want…I don't know. I guess I could use a friend right now. This is all a bit overwhelming."

Teo stopped abruptly and Emil had to backtrack.

"I am not your friend." Teo pointed a finger at Emil's chest. "You lied to me."

"I didn't lie. No one asked if I was human."

"You used…*mago*…magic. You fooled me. I have a mark on my record now because of you."

"I'm sorry, but it was necessary. I wanted to get inside Vioska, and that seemed the best way." He laid a hand on Teo's arm. Teo stared at it and frowned.

"And now that you are here, what will you do?"

"I…" That was a tricky question. Could he trust Teo with his true purpose? "I don't know."

Teo grunted a laugh. "When you find out, don't come looking for me." He pulled his arm away and stalked off.

THE FOLLOWING MORNING, A strange man woke him at dawn by pulling off his covers and kicking his bed frame.

"Get up. Get dressed. You are due in the *udwar* in fifteen minutes." The man's accent was thick and it took Emil's sleepy brain a moment to process. Before he could ask what *udwar* meant, he was alone again.

Five minutes later he was hastily dressed and on the street. He grabbed the first soldier he saw and asked, "Udwar?" The man looked at him like he was crazy, but pointed toward the town center. The dome of the Hall of Mages loomed over the rooftops, and Emil made his way toward that, assuming that *udwar* meant the mustering field in front of the hall.

He passed small shops just opening their doors for the day—knife sellers, tailors, and some barns for livestock. These would be to feed the krowa since the opji had no need for animal meat.

The journey also forced him to pass a dozen krowa pens.

So many! He'd known the opji were keeping hundreds, if not thousands of krowa, but knowing and seeing were two different experiences. Filthy, bleak faces stared at the activity passing them by. The opji ignored them. Emil tried to mimic this indifference, but his eyes were drawn to the hopeless stares.

As he entered the town square, he got his bearings. The Hall of Mages filled one entire side of the udwar. Dozens of soldiers had formed ranks and did exercises in the open square. A squad of wojaks paced around the perimeter, chaperoned by mages.

Pen Five was just ahead. He steeled himself to walk by it without a glance, and he almost made it.

"Emil!"

He froze. Stephen was pressed against the fence.

"Emil!" His grubby hands reached through the links, trying to grasp his sleeve. "Emil what happened?" Ray stood silently beside his brother. Emil's eyes locked on his and Ray nodded.

"I can't talk now, but I'll—"

"Janzek! Come here!"

Emil jerked toward the command like it was laced with magic. It came from the center of the square, near the stairs that led to the hall.

Stephen continued to cry his name and Ray shushed him. Emil walked away stiff-backed and fast.

"You're late!" barked an opji standing in front of a squad. The soldiers had stopped their exercises to watch the newcomer.

"My name is Ebbe. I am *Ormeza*. That means Sergeant to you. If you break the rules you will be punished. Talking to krowa is breaking the rules. Being late is breaking the rules. Do you understand, *ferdiek*?"

Emil had no idea what that last word meant, but by the way Ebbe sneered, it wasn't a compliment. He swallowed hard and nodded.

Ebbe pointed to the edge of the square and shouted "*Fut!*"

Emil looked to where he pointed and saw only the wojaks being put through their paces. He turned back to the sergeant, confused.

"*Fut!*" Ebbe shouted again. He made running motions with his fingers. Emil ran.

He did a lap around the square on the tail of the wojak squad and returned to Ebbe.

"Fut!" The sergeant pointed again. Emil ran some more. He ran until his legs felt like wet noodles and then returned to the sergeant, who only cried, "Fut!"

For hours he ran. The only benefit of this exercise was that he got to watch the wojaks up close. They weren't running to get fit or for punishment like Emil. They were running because a group of opji mages were being trained in the art of navigating them.

Left on their own, the wojaks would be overwhelmed by bloodlust, and they would tear through anything living—opji, human, fae or beast. No one outside of Vioska understood how the opji controlled them. So Emil watched and he ran, though he learned only that his keening wasn't strong enough to understand the magic used in wojak herding.

He ran for three days, through sleet and bitter cold. On the fourth day, Ebbe finally, grudgingly, allowed him to join the ranks of other soldiers. They spent the first hour practicing vigorous calisthenics. For the rest of the day, they paired off and fought one-on-one.

"No fangs," Ebbe warned him. Emil nodded. He'd been in a few brawls in his time and felt pretty sure he could hold his own. That confidence lasted for ninety seconds and disappeared in a puff of breath as his opponent slammed a fist into his solar plexus. Emil folded as his lungs emptied. The soldier slammed a fist on his spine. He heard bones crack.

The day only went downhill from there. These opji soldiers had been training to fight since childhood. They were well fed and well trained. Bout after bout, Emil found himself on the ground. Or hunched over, gasping for breath. Or kneeling in his own blood. The sergeant looked on with disgust each time he needed minutes to heal.

They broke for a rest at midday. Emil limped to his room and collapsed on the bed. Two hours later, he was back at it. Practice continued until the sun fell below the rooflines, casting the udwar in shadow.

Ebbe finally called a halt. Emil stared at the darkening sky after his last opponent laid him flat again.

The soldier loomed above, his lip curled in a sneer. "Krowa lover." He spat and a gob of saliva hit the dirt inches from Emil's face.

Every bone aching in his body, Emil pushed himself off the ground, thinking it wasn't a coincidence that when they wanted him to fail they spoke opji, but when they wanted their insults understood, they spoke perfect English.

Well, he wouldn't fail. He wouldn't give them the satisfaction.

That was the moment his mission shifted. Yes, he would still spy for Kyra and bring her the intel she needed to beat these fuckers, but now it was personal. Now he would beat them to prove that it was perfectly fine to be opji *and* a krowa lover.

The next week followed a similar pattern. Wake at dawn, exercise, spar, rest through the midday, spar some more, and fall into bed exhausted. By the sixth day, he was almost holding his own in the fights. At least he got in a few good hits before he went down, and his opponents no longer took his defeat for granted.

Every day he walked past Pen Five and studiously ignored Ray and Stephen. He could feel their eyes on him as he trained in the square.

During a water break, he turned his back on Pen Five so he wouldn't be tempted to communicate with Ray. Instead, he watched the novice mages run wojaks through their paces. One of the soldiers in his own squad, sat beside him and offered more water.

"My name is Voldi. You fought well today."

Emil hid his surprise. No one but the sergeant had spoken to him in a week.

"I am…Janzek." His opji name didn't roll off his tongue.

Voldi nodded. "I know who you are. Everyone knows. *Veszet baba*, they call you. The lost babe. Did you really grow up among the savage queen's court?"

"Yes. But Queen Leighna wasn't a savage."

Voldi frowned. "You should not say such things out loud. The wind has many ears." He tipped his fingers upward, a slight gesture that meant to encompass everyone around them.

Emil changed the subject by nodding toward the wojaks who were now climbing on top of each other to form a pyramid.

"They're amazing," he said. "I would love to learn what they do."

Voldi laughed. It was a harsh sound, as if he didn't do it often.

"You cannot even speak the language. You will never be a mage."

"Would you teach me? The language, I mean. And the rules. My mere existence seems to offend people. Maybe if I learned the basics…I don't know. Maybe I would fit in better."

Voldi studied him. He was big for an opji, tall and broad across the chest. His dark hair was trimmed short and it seemed to accentuate his blunt features.

Instead of answering, Voldi asked his own question.

"Is it true you survived on blood of pigs?"

Emil nodded. Voldi looked thoughtful. He leaned in and whispered. "Maybe that's why you don't visit the *kuchonya*?"

"Kuchonya?"

"The…I do not know your word. Eating place? Where food is served."

"The dining hall?"

"Yes, dining hall. You have not visited. It has been noted."

Voldi stopped there, but the threat was implied.

Emil was being watched. They knew he hadn't fed since the zycha. And if he didn't visit the *kuchonya* soon and drain the blood of a krowa, there would be repercussions.

"Thank you for letting me know. I will visit the…uh…kuchonya."

"Good." Voldi slapped Emil's knee. It was like being smacked by a two-by-four. "I will teach you. Tonight, after you feed. I will meet you in the kuchonya." He downed the last of his water and strode off, leaving Emil in the growing darkness.

11

The woman looked less scared than he felt. The feeding room was small and stuffy and bare except for a bed with black silk sheets and a dark red blanket. The walls were painted red too and had a satiny sheen like damask. The only illumination came from one brass sconce holding a single candle.

So many shadows to hide the stains.

The krowa lounged on the bed, looking bored. She was clean, but ragged around the edges. Her hair had been badly cut, fingernails chewed to nubs, and there were dark circles around her eyes. She wouldn't look at him. She just stared at the wall with a blank expression on her face.

Emil sat on the edge of the bed and fidgeted with the sheet. He'd drunk human blood before, during the zycha, of course, but also during his rebellious teen years, when he'd bought it on the black market. Back then, the blood had come in anonymous bags. It had been thrilling to think that the essence of a human coursed down his throat, but still, the whole thing had been quite sterile.

This full-fleshed human offering was anything but sterile.

"What's your name?" His voice seemed to fall into the shadows and disappear. She finally looked at him and cocked her head.

"Lara." She smiled. Her eyes were dead.

"Lara, I don't want to drink."

She shrugged and slid down into the bed as she lifted her thin shift to reveal that she was naked underneath. Naked and painfully thin. He grabbed her hand to stop her.

"No!" The word burst from him and she shrank away. "No," he said more gently. "Not that either."

Now the poor woman looked confused. Emil ran a trembling hand over his eyes.

He had to do this. Voldi waited outside. Others were watching. He had to play the good little opji boy.

"You're going to think this is crazy, but I've never actually fed from a person before. Would you help me?" It was a ridiculous request. Of course she wouldn't help him to violate her body and drink her lifeblood.

He met her gaze and held it. "I don't want to hurt you."

She scooted closer and held out her wrist. "Here. It hurts less when you drink here."

Emil stared at the pale wrist with enticing blue veins. He brought it to his lips and her scent washed over him—hot, musky and sweet. The bloodlust took over. He sank his fangs into her flesh and drank.

The world went dark red and fuzzy. When he came back to himself, he lay with his face pressed against the krowa's arm. He was crying.

"I'm sorry. I'm so sorry." He thrust the hand away, but Lara nudged it under his nose again.

"You must lick it, or it won't heal."

And so Emil washed the krowa's arm in tears and saliva.

Lara lay back with a beatific smile on her face. She waved her arms above her head in a slow, dancing pattern.

She's high on vampire venom. My venom.

Emil leaned over and retched, spilling his hard-won meal on the floor.

It seemed like hours later when he was finally composed enough to leave the chamber. Voldi met him with a clap on the back that send him stumbling a few steps.

His voice boomed. "The lost babe found his way home!"

Ichovidar had disavowed him as a son, but Emil didn't believe him. His mother had run from Vioska for a reason. His adopted fae mother had given him little information about her, only that her name was Tereza and she feared that Emil's father would take her child if she stayed. It seemed unlikely that Ichovidar would threaten to take a child that wasn't his.

As the days passed with no summons from the king, Emil realized that Ichovidar probably had dozens of bastards roaming around Vioska. What was one more?

Once he got over this fear of being singled out, Emil's days fell into an easy routine. Voldi was well-respected among the soldiers, and when they saw him mentoring Emil their antagonism relaxed.

His situation improved even more when the sergeant told him to join the archers for the day. Thanks to his impeccable education (courtesy of Lady Lughwaite), Emil was already proficient with a bow. The opji weapons were bigger and heavier, but the zycha had also improved his strength, and he had no trouble hitting the target. His instructor was impressed and immediately switched Emil to the archery division.

He still had to train with Ebbe in the mornings, but now he spent his afternoons at target practice. His evenings were for Voldi, who drilled him on opji vocabulary and started him on easy readers.

Emil picked up the language fast, but Voldi wasn't surprised.

"You heard it while you were in your mother's womb." He touched his head and heart in a gesture that Emil had come to recognize. It was the opji way of honoring their ancestors.

"The language is part of you as much as her blood," he said. Even so, he was pleased when Emil graduated from children's books to opji histories.

Emil spent every evening in the great library in the Hall of Mages, digesting every bit of opji lore he could find. He also watched mages come and go from the library, and once, Ichovidar appeared. He seemed surprised to see Emil, but they didn't speak. That lack of attention from his biological father both relieved and irritated Emil in ways that he didn't want to examine too closely.

The mages eventually grew used to seeing him sitting quietly at a table with an open book, and they began to speak freely in his presence.

Emil's opji was now good enough to understand most of what they said. He heard them talk about summoning demons and knew it wasn't just theory. He'd seen the demon they kept in a cage behind the hall.

They also spoke of something called *brechzen*, which Emil translated as "the breaking." It was a new rite Ichovidar was working on. Emil didn't understand the alchemical specifics, but they were very excited about it, and spoke with animated gestures as they poured over ancient texts.

During this time, Emil learned the history of his people. It was a history steeped in blood and magic. For millennia, while human magic was infantile, the opji had reared powerful mages. But their numbers were never great, and they'd often fought for the simple right to exist. Humans had nearly annihilated them several times. These near genocides had colored the opji world view and turned them into a military race. Every legendary hero, every story they told their children, revolved around a fight to death—a fight for the right to exist.

The Flood wars had boosted opji magic. It had also given magic to the humans and brought powerful fae into their world. Then Terra intervened and secluded the humans and fae behind wards. Once again the opji found themselves fighting for their very existence.

Emil found himself thinking about these histories while he lay in his cot at night. The struggles the opji faced century after century...they almost made him sympathize. Almost. At least he now understood why they viewed the rest of the world with such fear and hatred. He wondered if there could ever be a reconciliation between the opji and Terra's other inhabitants.

On a winter's evening in early February, Emil opened a biography of Vidar, the opji whose weapon had led him here. It was written by Ichovidar. That was interesting. He outlined Vidar's original krowa system, the idea that opji could breed their food instead of hunt and scrape for it. Vidar's proposal had been radical at the time. Many thought that farming humans would make the opji weak. Vidar countered that it would make them strong because they would never lack for blood and they could turn their attention to training their army instead of hunting.

And that's exactly what they did. The treatise continued to modern day, and Vidar was proven right in one respect. The stable feeding had made the opji strong. Their numbers swelled. What Vidar hadn't anticipated was the frailty of the humans. The final chapter of the treatise outlined all the ways that humans in captivity died—disease, malnutrition, and fighting among themselves. It was even noted that some humans appeared to die of simple melancholy, a concept the opji found difficult to understand. The author surmised that radical policies would have to be adopted in order to keep the krowa population healthy and abundant.

The candles in the library had burned low when Emil finished the book. He glanced at the publication date. It was nearly ten years ago, about the same time the opji started raiding homesteads and taking captives in bigger numbers.

It seemed those radical policies were never put in place, and the opji had been forced to increase their krowa the old fashioned way. He turned to the last page and read Ichovidar's final lines again, translating as best he could.

The human and fae colonies will never accept opji supremacy. That leaves only one choice for the continuation of our race: the brechzen.

There it was again. The breaking. Emil closed the book. It was near dawn and he was alone in the library. He knew he should get some rest. If he was late for mustering, Ebbe would make him run laps all morning. But he needed to know more about this brechzen.

He went back to the stacks, but this time, instead of heading for the history section, he picked up one of the alchemy books a group of mages had been excitedly debating earlier in the evening, and he began to read.

The weeks passed. Emil kept his head down. He trained. He studied. Once a week, he drank krowa blood, just enough to keep him alive. And eventually, he felt the eyes of his watchers turn away. He was no longer a novelty or a threat.

On his way to the library one evening, he slipped a note into Ray's hand as he passed Pen Five. It told Ray not to give up hope, because he was finding a way to free him. And it warned Ray to burn the note immediately.

CHAPTER

12

Emil was low opji in the pecking order. He still lost fights in the training ring every day. He was better with the bow, but still not one of the top ranking archers. But one thing he did better than any opji was sneak around unnoticed. The opji preferred brute force to stealth. Emil had been slinking through the shadows of Montreal all his life.

During his off hours, he walked the streets of Vioska, learning every back alley and escape route. He counted the barracks and estimated the number of soldiers Ichovidar could put in the field. He loitered in the gardens behind the Hall of Mages, where undead ogres were kept in a reinforced pen. There were twelve of them, and they each stood head and shoulders above the opji mages that controlled them. The ogres made Emil's skin crawl. Undead humans were bad enough, and ogres were somehow worse. But even those monsters couldn't keep his attention in this back garden. Not when a demon lounged next to their pen in a twelve foot cube made of wood and iron. The cage had to be heavily warded because otherwise a demon of that size could easily break out. The creature's eyes followed him as he passed through the garden, and her gaze left him feeling oily and sour.

Leaving the garden of monsters—as he'd come to call it—he headed along the alleys that paralleled the udwar, poking his nose into every corner, not really knowing what he was looking for.

He avoided the krowa pens, and Pen Five in particular. His self-discipline wasn't good enough to stop him from talking to Ray and Stephen. Best to take the temptation out of the equation.

Past the stables, he stopped when he spied two opji conferring. It was Teo and Voldi.

Emil hung back in the shadows and watched. The first time he'd seen Teo and Voldi together, he'd thought nothing of it. The second time could have been a coincidence. But this was the third time, and he took notice.

Soldiers were not encouraged into friendships. Walk into any tavern in the city and you'd find solitary drinkers, brooding over cups of *diszwin,* a mulled wine mixed with animal blood favored by the opji.

Besides, there was something off about their stance, like each was about to flee. Teo kept glancing nervously up the alley.

Way to be cool, guys. Why don't you just scream it out loud—we're up to no good!

The opji concluded their clandestine transaction and parted ways. Emil waited a few minutes, then followed Teo.

Near midnight on an early spring day in March, he slipped out of his barracks unnoticed. Twice already, he'd followed Teo to a small cottage on the edge of town. He had a feeling about that cottage and Teo's late night assignations. Was he meeting a lover? Doubtful. Teo was up to something and Emil planned to find out what.

The cottage was in an older part of town. The buildings on either side were abandoned. Across the street lived an elderly opji woman whose lights were out long before the midnight visitors started to arrive.

Emil crouched beside a rain barrel in her yard, making himself as small as possible to fit inside the shadow.

Teo arrived first. He paused at the door to the cottage, looking up the lane way before slipping inside. Eight more opji, five men and three women arrived at intervals. Their movements were quick and sure. No lights went on inside the cottage and the door was well oiled to make no noise.

Voldi was the last to arrive.

Emil crept across the lane into the shadows between the target cottage and the abandoned one next door. A cat hissed at him for disturbing its nightly hunt and Emil showed it his fangs. The cat yowled then grudgingly slunk off.

The voices inside paused, then continued, too low for him to make out words. He crept along the alley, placing each footstep on damp earth and not leaves or twigs. An ill-fitting door on the back side of the cottage was nearly crumbling in its frame, and it let him peer inside. It was all darkness. But from here, the voices were clear. He heard that word again. *Brechzen,* the breaking.

A male voice he didn't recognize said, "I don't want to leave Vioska. This is my home."

A woman answered. "Don't be a baby. If we must leave, we leave."

Voldi said, "Opji are nomads. We have been for thousands of years. Ichovidar's krowa experiment failed. We must move on."

"But the Inbetween!" The male voice said, then hissed as if he faced an enemy. "It will kill us just the same."

There was some dissension at that, murmurs for and against leaving Vioska.

"Voldi speaks true," Teo said. "We were never meant to settle like a clan in one place. It goes against our nature. We must take our families and leave this place. The Inbetween is dangerous, but it is also full of opportunity."

Emil stood with his back to the cottage and his ear pressed to the gap in the door. He'd found them. The dissenters that he knew had to be in Vioska somewhere.

Finally, another male voice spoke up. This one, Emil recognized. It was Nikinor, one of the mages he often ran into at the library.

"Running away isn't an option. If Ichovidar performs the breaking, we won't be able to run far enough."

"We will take a ship," said a woman. "Sail for the old world." The room paused as everyone considered her suggestion.

"You are not listening." Nikinor's frustration sounded in his tone. "Running won't help. Nowhere will be safe. If Ichovidar breaks open the veil, the very fabric of time and space will be shattered. Demons will come through and worse. Things we cannot even imagine. And it won't just be an invasion. A tear in the veil of this size will crush our natural laws. Time might be turned inside out. The moon could be pulled from the sky. There is no telling the extent of the disaster."

Emil realized a second too late that Nikinor's voice was getting louder. The door was shoved open. It smashed into his temple and he stumbled back. Hands grabbed him. A rag was shoved into his mouth. They hauled him inside. Someone bound his wrists behind him and he was pushed into a chair.

There was barely enough light to make out the figures seated around the room.

"How much did you hear?" Nikinor asked. Emil couldn't answer with the gag and he shrugged.

"It doesn't matter," said the woman. "He's seen our faces. We should kill him."

"This is Janzek," Teo said. "The lost babe. I think we should hear what he has to say before we kill him."

That was only mildly comforting.

Nikinor leaned toward him and pressed a blade to his throat. "If you scream, I will kill you."

Emil swallowed hard and nodded. Nikinor removed the filthy rag from his mouth.

"Why are you here? Who do you report to?"

"No one. I'm here on my own."

"Why?" He pressed the blade against Emil's throat.

"I…I was looking for you. Not you in particular, but someone who…" He paused. Should he lay it all out? What did he have to lose, except his life? "I came looking for dissenters. Like me."

The room was silent.

Nikinor relaxed and the blade moved away from Emil's throat. He took that as a good sign and continued in a hurried tone.

"I heard you. You don't believe in the krowa system. Neither do I. It's an abomination. And it's not sustainable. I think you know that. I lived in Montreal for twenty-nine years without drinking human blood…mostly." They didn't have to know about his rebellious teen years. "We can live together with the humans and fae, work with them."

One of the women scoffed. "He's a fool. And Ichovidar's bastard. Why should we listen to anything he has to say."

"Because he is also Tereza's son," Voldi said. "We owe her that much." He turned to Emil. "We are the *Bunters*. Your mother was a founding member of this group." He touched his head and heart. "She and Nikinor were the first ones to understand that something has to change in Vioska or we will all perish."

Emil stared at Nikinor. "You knew my mother?" There was no way to say those words without sounding like a lost little boy, and Emil didn't even try.

Nikinor nodded. "She was my cousin. When Ichovidar took an interest in her, my family despaired. Even back then, he was too powerful to deny. But Tereza confirmed what I had already suspected. Ichovidar is mad. He has lost the filter that lets normal people discern right from wrong. And even worse, he has become obsessed with magic. It has twisted him. He no longer recognizes that his plans go against the basic laws of nature. He will kill us all."

"But you'll stop him," Emil said. "You must."

Nikinor leaned back in his chair. In the gloom, Emil couldn't make out his features. When he spoke, the voice seemed to come from the darkness. "That is what we were debating. Do we stay and fight, or do we run."

"I will fight," Emil said. "Let me help you."

There was a long moment of silence. Teo finally broke it.

"He comes from the krowa pens. He has friends there. We have been trying for months to make allies within the krowa, with no success. He might be useful."

"I also have friends in Montreal." Emil wouldn't tell them about Kyra and the army coming their way. Not yet. "You will need allies if you defeat Ichovidar. I can help."

A woman swore and shook her head, but the silence of the others seemed to be in his favor.

"You must swear a blood oath," Nikinor said. "If you betray us, the magic will kill you."

"Fine. Whatever."

Nikinor sliced through the ropes tying his hands, and said, "Take off your jacket."

It was cold enough to freeze, but Emil removed his coat.

"Roll up your sleeve."

When his flesh was revealed, Nikinor sliced an X on his forearm. Emil braced himself not to pull away. Nikinor chanted over the blood welling from the cut.

"Now, swear on the blood of your own heart that you will take your life before betraying your fellow Bunters."

"I swear." Emil was starting to shake from the cold.

"Say it!"

"I swear that I will kill myself before betraying the Bunters." He tried to speak with conviction, though he felt a bit silly, like they were kids playing at super secret spy.

Nikinor spat on the cut, and Emil felt a jolt go through him as the oath was sealed with magic.

Things just got real.

The cut was already healing when Nikinor handed him the rag that had gagged him. He wiped away the blood.

The others had stood and they all watched him.

He pulled on his coat and said, "Now what?"

"Now you go home and sleep," Voldi said. "We will get word to you when we meet again."

13

Things started to move quickly after that meeting. A call to muster went through the barracks in early April. Emil had been in Vioska too long. He'd promised Kyra he'd return by the end of March, but there were only two gates through the ward, and they were both guarded. He'd already made an attempt to get through with a flimsy excuse that he was going hunting. That had landed him a reprimand from Ebbe and two days of cleaning horse stalls. It turned out that heightened opji senses meant horse dung was particularly offensive.

When the call to arms came, Emil knew this was his chance to get outside the ward. Once in the Inbetween he would make a run for it.

He dressed quickly and joined the ranks of soldiers heading toward the town center. He drew up beside one of his many sparring partners.

"What's going on?"

The soldier didn't look at him. "We attack Montreal. Finally."

A zing of surprise and fear thrummed through Emil. "But their ward. It's impenetrable."

"Maybe so, but their farms and their barracks are outside the ward and weak. We will kill many of theirs." His voice was flat. He was neither excited or scared.

They're drones, Emil thought. Worker bees being sent from the hive to kill or be killed.

In the square, he joined the ranks of his squad. Hundreds of soldiers stood at silent attention. Mage soldiers waited at the wojak pens.

The door to the Hall of Mages opened and Ichovidar stepped out. Emil got one good look before he dropped his gaze to the ground like the rest of his squad, but he saw Ichovidar pause at the top of the stairs and assess his troops.

He expected a call to arms or a rousing pep talk, but Ichovidar descended the stairs without a word. He strode up the aisle of soldiers with his mages flocked around him. When he reached the far end of the square, the squads turned and followed.

"Not you." A hand grabbed Emil's shoulder. Ebbe jerked him out of formation. "You stay."

"But…" Emil stared after his squad, then turned to Ebbe. "Why?"

The sergeant's lip curled. "Because I don't trust you."

And there it was. It didn't matter that he had done nothing to earn that distrust. He was the veszet baba, the lost babe. And he always would be. He didn't fit in here anymore than he did in Montreal.

"Report to Kanwa. You are under his command until I return." Ebbe turned and followed the squads through the city. Emil thought about trying to sneak out with the soldiers, but Ebbe had probably warned the gate guards.

He sighed and went looking for Kanwa, the master of the stables. He'd be shoveling horse shit for the rest of the week.

THE RETURNING ARMY HAD a distinctly different feel. The squads swept into the city with an air of triumph, leading a horde of new recruits for the krowa pens.

Ichovidar went straight to the Hall of Mages and locked himself inside his laboratory.

Several times during the next hours, Emil heard that term, the brechzen—the breaking. It was whispered in taverns and in the mess hall which was busy as soldiers fed after the battle and long march. From overheard conversations, Emil understood that the attack on the shanty town south of Montreal and the Hub barracks had been a success, and more importantly, Ichovidar had found whatever he'd been looking for—the last ingredient that would let him begin the brechzen.

The following day, he sparred with Voldi, and lost as usual. While Voldi had him pinned, he whispered one word in his ear. "Midnight."

It was time for the Bunters to act.

Emil showed no reaction, but only heaved the bigger man upward and rolled out from under him.

He felt a new vitality. Things were happening. Hub would not stand by and take an outright assault from the opji. Montreal would be mustering too. The fae, the humans, the alchemists. They'd be coming.

Kyra would be coming.

The thought energized him and for the first time since taking the zycha rite, Emil won a fight against another opji. He laid his sparring partner flat and hissed into his face, showing off his fangs. The soldier flinched, and Emil couldn't deny it. He felt strong.

THAT NIGHT THE BUNTERS met in the abandoned cottage on the edge of town. The feeling of impending action infected their small group too.

A man named Alek pushed again for them to leave. The woman who had taken an instant dislike to Emil spoke out against this plan. Her name was Beda, and she watched everyone with overt suspicion.

"Why should we leave now?" she demanded. "Maybe Ichovidar was right all this time. Maybe we can break their ward and take what is rightfully ours."

This brought a wave of comments from the others, some for and some against the idea of invasion. Emil held his tongue. He was too new to the group to foist his opinions on them.

"You're a fool," Teo said. "And you don't even know enough to know what a fool you are. Nikinor has made it clear that running isn't an option."

Beda straightened in her chair and crossed her arms.

"And where is Nikinor? If this is so important, why isn't he here to back us up?"

"The brechzen has begun. Ichovidar will fast for three days and then begin the rite. The Zaubers have all been called in to pray over him while he fasts. Nikinor told me to warn you. If we are going to intervene, we must act soon."

"But what can we do?" Beda asked.

"We could kill him." This came from Hanzel, the one who spoke the least in these meetings. His quiet, calm voice seemed to hold weight.

"That would be suicide," Teo said. "The Zaubers guard him. We'd have to fight through their ranks."

Emil decided it was time to speak up.

"We'll have help. The humans and the fae are coming. I know for a fact that an army is already on its way."

"How do you know?" Voldi said.

This was it. He would either sway them to his cause or they would call him a traitor and kill him.

"Because I was sent here by a delegation of humans and fae."

"But you are opji!" Beda spoke a little too loudly. She lowered her voice. "How can you work with those animals? They are no better than the krowa."

Emil opened his mouth to answer, but Teo cut him off. "The krowa are not animals. A hundred years ago, we lived among them."

"But always apart," snapped Beda.

"Only because we kept ourselves apart. There are ways for us to live with humans as a community. Janzek is proof of that. Even without the zycha, he was able to control his bloodlust and thrive. And there will always be humans willing to give up their blood for the right price."

"The right price." Beda snorted. "Do you mean money or simply for the high?"

"Either."

Emil shifted in his seat. He thought of Lara that first time he fed, and how she faded into a stupor of pleasure from his venom. The idea that she was addicted to vampire venom still made guilt rise like gorge in his throat.

"Addicting humans may not be the best answer," he said. "But we can live together. Live and thrive. Can you say the same thing about living under Ichovidar's rule? I have been here for only a few weeks, but I can tell you the opji are already beaten. Ichovidar has a whip to your backs, but you are so used to the misery, you don't even feel it anymore. There is more to life than training to fight."

A voice came from outside and everyone in the room fell silent. The sound of boots on cobblestones echoed through the night. Emil's gaze darted around the small room, looking for a place to hide, but there was none. The cottage was abandoned and bare.

The Bunters sat in frozen silence. Outside the footsteps grew louder, stopped, and moved on. After a moment, Teo nodded toward Hanzel and the man slipped out the back door. Minutes later he returned.

"A patrol. They're gone now, but there are patrols all over."

This was bad news. The guards never bothered with this derelict part of town. If Ichovidar was sending patrols even into the slums, it meant he was leaving nothing to chance. It meant he was ready for whatever came next.

By silent agreement, the Bunters dispersed, slinking into the night one after the other. No plans were made to meet again.

14

mil lay in his bed but couldn't sleep. He rose and peered out the window. A patrol of four guards marched by in the street below. He froze, not wanting to attract their gaze. The guards rounded the corner but still he watched the road. Ten minutes later, more soldiers marched by.

The patrols, while a nuisance, gave him some relief. The patrol by the abandoned cottage hadn't meant the Bunters were in danger of discovery. It only meant Ichovidar was leaving nothing to chance while he finalized his plans.

It also meant that it was time to run.

The Bunters could argue amongst themselves until Kyra's army fell on them, but he needed to get out. Now.

And he needed to steal back whatever artifact Ichovidar had brought home to fuel the breaking.

He had no clock in his room. Soldiers weren't allowed such luxuries, but by the look of the sky to the east, dawn wasn't far off. And then he'd be expected in the training yard. Already, he could hear voices in the street as soldiers came to feed before training.

It was too late to slip away. He'd have to wait until the midday lull. Everyone would be tired from training and sunlight would drive them indoors.

He lay back on his cot and waited for the morning summons.

A COLD WIND BLEW from the north. Emil stuck his hands under his arms to keep his fingers from freezing. Training had ended a half hour ago, and any warmth he'd built up sparring had long seeped from his blood.

They hadn't been dismissed yet. Row upon row of fighters stood at the ready, eyes straight ahead and locked on the door to the Hall of Mages.

And they waited.

Emil held back a fidget. No one else moved and he couldn't draw the sergeant's attention. The minutes dragged on. Overhead, the sun beat down.

He glanced toward the lane leading out of the city. Could he make a run for it? No. One shout from the sergeant and he'd be tackled by dozens of soldiers. He was too late to stop whatever was coming.

Finally, the doors opened. Emil expected Ichovidar to emerge, ready to proclaim his intent to break the world in two. Instead, a mage stepped out and conferred with the others already gathered by the doors.

Something had happened. He could tell by the way the mages bunched together, leaning in so their words weren't overheard. They broke up and headed back inside, all except for one who signaled to the training marshal, who in turn, signaled to the sergeants.

Ebbe whistled for their attention. "The humans and fae are on the move! Their army approaches. Go get some rest, and be back here at the fourth hour! Tonight we face our enemy!"

A cheer rose up. It was the most emotion Emil had ever heard from the soldiers.

The ranks broke up. Hunger and sunlight would drive them inside. He'd have four hours to find the artifact Ichovidar was using to fuel his mad spell and then get out of Vioska.

But first he had to say goodbye.

He followed the general flow of traffic toward the barracks but slipped inside a barn until the street was empty. Then he backtracked. The high sun didn't leave many shadows to hide in and he had to hug the edge of a building until he made it to the corner of Pen Five.

A woman sat with her back to the chain links, trying to glean a bit of warmth from the sun. He poked her and she startled.

"Hush! I won't hurt you. Get Raymond." The woman goggled at him. "Quickly!"

Ray had already seen him. His long fingers slipped through the links to cover Emil's.

"You shouldn't be here," he hissed.

"I know. But I had to." Irrational and unwelcome emotion choked him. What was this man to him, really? They'd shared their warmth at night, shared their food and water. But that was all. And now he was risking everything—his life and the success of his mission—to say goodbye.

But then he looked into Ray's eyes and saw his own longing reflected there. Longing and understanding. And yes, love. And he knew he'd risk all that and more for this man.

"I have to go." The words came out in a croak.

"I know."

"Kyra's army is close by, I swear. Tell Liam." Emil swallowed hard against the lump in his throat. "I'll come back. I promise."

"I know." Ray's gaze never wavered. His grip tightened on Emil's fingers and it felt like they squeezed his barely-beating heart.

Ray let go and stood back from the fence. Emil felt like a captured pigeon released into the wild but not sure he wanted to fly.

His eyes blurred. He turned and stumbled.

Right into Ebbe.

The sergeant's eyes were hard, his lips pressed thin.

Excuses for talking to the krowa tumbled through Emil's mind, but none of them made it to his lips.

"Take him," Ebbe said, and Emil noticed the other two soldiers lurking in the alley. They grabbed his arms and jerked him off his feet. His boots dragged on the road as they dragged him away, and the sound of Raymond screaming his name faded.

Ebbe had warned him. You break the rules, you pay. Emil didn't bother to plead his case. Not yet, anyway. Maybe this arrest was a good thing. Eventually, they'd bring him before someone in power, maybe even Ichovidar. He'd make his move then.

They threw him in a cell. It was near pitch black, with only a bit of torch light coming through a barred window on the door. There were two cots in the cell and nothing else.

At first he thought he was alone, until a mound of blankets on one cot stirred and moaned.

Emil backed against the wall. Slowly his eyes adjusted to the gloom. The man in the cot sat up.

It was Nikinor.

Bruises darkened both his eyes. His lip was split and swollen. Opji healed unnaturally fast. Bruises and cuts took only minutes to fade. Broken bones might take hours. Emil had never seen an opji with bruises.

"They drugged me." Nikinor's words were slurred. "Blocked my healing, so they could…" He coughed and Emil heard wetness in his lungs. "So they could torture me. No fun torturing someone who heals too quickly." He coughed again, and Emil realized he was laughing.

Had he gone mad? Had the mages beaten him for so long that his mind snapped?

Nikinor seemed to rally a bit. He sat up straighter and spat on the floor.

"I'm sorry I had to bring you into this. I thought about giving up Beda… she's such a…*ferdiek* anyway." He laughed wetly again.

The truth was dawning inside Emil. "Give up Beda?" His arrest wasn't about him talking to Ray after all.

"I had to give them a name, and it had to be you. If someone was going to betray Vioska it would be the lost babe, wouldn't it?"

"They captured you! They know about the Bunters."

Nikinor nodded. "They know there is dissent in Vioska. They don't know that we are organized."

"Organized?" Emil let out a snort and slumped on the second cot. "You aren't organized. You can barely agree on how to tie your shoes, let alone how to lead Vioska away from disaster."

"Maybe so, but at least we try. At least we acknowledge the need for change."

"It's not enough." Emil leaned against the stone wall. It had all gone to shit. Everything. He should have gotten away weeks ago. He shouldn't have even come. He knew next to nothing about the opji. Nothing that would help Kyra. And now he was the scapegoat for a bunch of ineffectual dissenters.

"It's for the best," Nikinor rasped. "The others will continue with our work."

Did this guy believe Teo and Voldi and Beda would make a difference? Really?

"If I can do anything to help, I will," Nikinor said.

"Just leave me alone," Emil growled. "You've done enough."

He tucked his knees against his chest and wrapped his arms around them. And he waited for his fate to be decided.

It was a long wait. Hours went by. Nikinor slept and when he woke, his bruises had finally faded. Nobody came to feed them or to speak to them, but voices could be heard regularly in the hall outside their cell. They were in the armory and soldiers came and went, collecting weapons.

"Somethings happening." Nikinor had his eye pressed to the one small window in the door.

After their first exchange, Emil had refused to talk to him, but when the flurry of activity outside quieted, he couldn't deny his curiosity.

He rose from the cot. His legs were stiff from the long hours of sitting.

"Someone's coming." Nikinor stepped back and waved at Emil to stand away from the door, as if it might explode inward. The lock turned. The door opened. And the light shone on Teo standing in the open doorway.

"Come! We must hurry!"

15

Teo led them to the armory at the end of the hall.

"Take a weapon."

Emil paused at the rack of swords. He preferred a bow.

"Anything!" Teo hissed. "You won't be using it. The wojaks stand outside the ward with four squads of archers and another four of infantry."

"Do we fight?" Emil chose a bow, a quiver of arrows, and two knives for his belt.

"We stall." Teo's sneer showed what he thought of those tactics. "The humans and fae gather, but Ichovidar refuses to attack."

"Why not?"

"He's waiting for the full moon," Nikinor said. "Tomorrow night he will commence the breaking. He doesn't need to defeat the enemy. He only needs to hold them off until then."

The breaking. It was really going to happen. Finally, Emil had information that was vital to Kyra's cause. She couldn't know that Armageddon was only a few hours away. She might stall for time—wait for her forces to gather. And that would be their ruin.

He had to get out of Vioska now and warn her that time was up.

They exited the armory by a back door. It was a damp, foggy morning. Nikinor left them, and Emil didn't try to stop him.

"Get to the gate," Teo said. "The guard on duty is one of ours. He'll let you through. And when the fighting starts, get away."

"And what will you do?" Emil asked.

Teo looked away.

"You have to do something! The Bunters could change the whole direction of this war!"

Teo hissed. "Do not speak so!"

Emil didn't care who heard them anymore. The city was about to be crushed between two armies. No one would care about a few dissenters.

Emil gripped Teo's arm. "Promise me you'll try. Convince the others. When the fighting begins, set something on fire so I'll know you got through to them. The armory! It's full of explosives. Blow it up, if you have to. And when the Montreal army comes through, I will let them know you are on our side."

"You can speak for the humans?" Teo asked.

Emil didn't hesitate. "I can speak for their general. Kyra Greene is fair. And tough. She'll wipe out the entire opji army to stop an invasion of Montreal. But she won't slaughter innocents."

Teo shook his head. "We are none of us innocent, my friend."

"But we are not killers. Please, Teo. Think about it. Convince the others before it's too late."

"I will, but you must go. Now!"

Emil stumbled along the alley. The armory was behind the Hall of Mages, near the garden of monsters. The demon's cage was gone. The ogre pens were empty. Ichovidar had moved all his weapons to the front lines.

He's showing off. Look how big my army of undead is. Look at my mighty demon.

It wouldn't matter. Emil really did know Kyra, and by now she'd have gathered an army three times the size of what the opji could put in the field.

He stopped as he came up against the back corner of the Hall of Mages.

But no army could stop the breaking, not once Ichovidar put it into motion. And then the veil between worlds would shatter. Demons would run free. Hell creatures of all kinds would invade. The very life-blood of their planet would be sucked dry.

He looked up at the building. In the pale morning light it didn't look like the place the world would end. It looked like a government building—where you got your driver's license or paid for parking tickets. But somewhere inside, was the catalyst that Ichovidar would use to break open the world.

He had to find it. He had no idea what he was looking for, but a good idea where to find it. Ichovidar would keep it close, somewhere he could easily protect it. Somewhere like his private study.

He left the bow and arrows under a bush and slipped inside the hall. The armory wasn't the only place that was deserted. He spied guards standing in front of two massive doors, but they were the only other souls in the building.

Everyone's at the front lines. Ichovidar wants to be alone to work his deadly magic.

That worked in Emil's favor. He headed in the other direction, seeing no one else until he reached the private office where he'd first met his bio dad.

The door was locked, but Emil jerked the handle and broke it.

Sometimes vampire strength came in handy.

He slipped inside and shut the door. The curtains were drawn but enough light seeped around their edges that he could make out the outline of the desk, chair and couch where he'd first seen Ichovidar.

On a shelf behind the desk, he spotted the Thorn of Vidar. Ichovidar had a wood display rack made for it, and the blade was the centerpiece of his bookcase.

Not for long.

Emil stepped around the desk, fully intending to take the thorn, if for no other reason than it would piss off Ichovidar, but his foot jammed up against a box, and a bolt of hot magic swept through him.

He jumped back, shaking his foot like it was on fire.

It was a cage, not a box, and heavily warded.

Two big brown eyes stared at him from inside the cage. A liver-colored, three-pronged nose snuffled at the bars without getting too close.

"Shar!"

Emil crouched. He reached for the cage and the ward zapped him again.

"Gods dammit!" He sucked on his finger, then shook it out. He sat back on his heels and studied the cage and its prisoner. The little creature stared back at him with big, scared eyes.

Dread hit him in a cold wave.

Kyra would never let Shar go. Ichovidar would have to pry the shar-lil from her dead fingers.

This is what he'd gone to Montreal for. This was what all the excitement was about. Shar was the fuel for the breaking.

But Kyra couldn't be dead. It wasn't possible. And until he had confirmation otherwise, he was going to assume that she was the one standing across from Ichovidar's army.

That was more likely. She would come for Shar.

"I wish I could take you to her little one." He reached for the cage again, testing the ward, but it was no use. The magic was too volatile.

He lay nearly flat on the floor so he could look Shar in the eye. "Hold tight, okay? Kyra's coming. I'm going to bring her right here and we'll get you out of there."

The little creature made a chirping noise. Emil didn't know how much she understood. But he could wait no longer.

He stood up and grabbed the Thorn of Vidar before letting himself out.

EMIL MINGLED WITH THE squads of soldiers on the front lines, keeping his head down and staying well away from Ebbe or anyone who might recognize him. Hazy clouds kept the sun from blinding them, but let through enough light to put the full might of the wojak army on display. The undead creatures were not organized like the opji archers who ranged behind them. They mingled and seethed, full of restless and insatiable energy. A group of mages surrounded them, hanging onto their invisible leashes.

The demon roared in its cage. The undead ogres echoed it with their own cries.

Behind him, Emil could feel the immense magic of Vioska's ward. They were outside its protection, while Ichovidar hid within. He knew the humans and fae would eventually break down the ward, but they'd have to fight through a thousand wojaks first. He was betting they wouldn't do it in time.

Because they didn't know the clock was running out. Only he could get that vital information to Kyra.

Someone rode into the burned out field some five hundred meters away. Even with his enhanced opji vision, Emil couldn't make out faces. There were four horses, at least. Maybe more hiding in the trees behind them.

No one moved. The enemies watched each other over the blackened ground.

A crow cawed in the distance, followed by the long "Arroooo" of a hound.

Emil knew that hound.

Was it possible?

Yes, it was.

That was no crow. And no ordinary hound. A massive creature launched into the sky. Thunderbird flew across the open field with a hell hound zipping around him.

"Shoot it!" A sergeant screamed. The archers raised their weapons and fired. Emil let his arrow go far to the right, with no chance of hitting anyone.

Thunderbird flew too high, but no one called a cease fire and hundreds of arrows were wasted in the futile attack. While all eyes were on the giant bird, Emil pushed his way to the front of the force. He dropped his bow at the edge of the wojak squads.

"Hey!" A mage called out. "What are you doing?"

At the same moment, Thunderbird beat his wings, sending a concussion through the army that flattened wojaks and opji in a wave. Emil had been expecting it and he recovered in time to see one of the undead ogres being plucked up in huge talons.

Oh, Raven. What are you up to?

Whatever it was, Emil used the confusion to slink even further toward the front lines.

More arrows flew after Thunderbird. Everyone watched as the talons released their prey and the ogre cascaded down. Someone ran from the tree line to finish it off.

Thunderbird landed and seemingly disappeared.

But Emil knew he only shifted back into the shape of a boy.

And if Raven was here, so was Kyra.

The squads were in an upheaval. No one had expected such a sudden and brutal attack. They were questioning all their tactics, wondering how many of those thunderbirds the human-fae army could put in the field.

Emil took advantage of the confusion.

The only way forward was through the pack of wojaks. They snarled and snapped at him, but whatever geas the mages used to keep the beasts from attacking opji held. He passed through their ranks unmolested and sprinted into the field.

There was a moment of shocked silence, then a call went up to fire.

He heard the distinctive twang of hundreds of arrows being released. Arrows smacked the dirt all around him. The sound of his own blood pounded in his ears. More arrows sailed overhead.

Something hit his shoulder, taking his breath away. He went down as his foot snagged on a charred log. His hands hit the ground and sunk into wet ash. He sucked in a breath.

Get up. Don't look back.

He looked back. An arrow stuck out of his shoulder. The pain hit him at the same moment.

Get up. Get up!

The voice screaming inside his head wasn't his own. It was Ray's.

Emil stood. The pain was shocking. It nearly immobilized him.

Run! came the voice again.

He ran. For Ray. And Stephen. And Teo. And for Kyra, Mason, Raven and that drooling hound who stood on the edge of the field, waiting for him to come home.

He stumbled over the last few meters of burned out ground and collapsed.

"I thought you'd never come." His voice rasped, and the last thing he saw before darkness took him was Kyra's stunned face. He'd made it. He was safe. Then he passed out.

*

Dear Reader,

Thorn of Vioska is my thank-you book for all the readers who stuck with Kyra through nine novels and four novellas. You cannot know how grateful I am that readers enjoyed these stories and kept asking for more. It meant that I could finally make my dream to be a full-time writer true. It meant that I found readers who feel the same feels as I do, who love critters of all kinds as much as I do, and who fill my life with joy and connections.

Reader wrangler rule #1: Always thank your readers and remember how blessed you are to have them.

So thank you.

Kim McDougall

Connect with Kim McDougall

Subscribe to Kim McDougall's newsletter (at KimMcDougall.com) to get the latest release updates, book deals and insider insights into novel creations. Plus, get 3 free eBooks just for subscribing. If you enjoyed this book I would be grateful for your honest review. It can be as short as you like. Even a few positive words will go a long way.

Other places you can follow Kim McDougall Books:

Facebook: https://www.facebook.com/KimMcDougallBooks

Instagram: https://www.instagram.com/kimmcdougallbooks

Amazon: https://www.amazon.com/-/e/B002C7CI2M

Bookbub: https://www.bookbub.com/authors/kim-mcdougall

Goodreads: https://www.goodreads.com/author/show/1432797.Kim_McDougall

Want to find out more about Kyra's world?

Learn more about the Valkyrie Bestiary series and other books by Kim McDougall at https://kimmcdougall.com.

Poke around at Kyra's blog at http://valkyriebestiary.com.

Find all the Valkyrie Bestiary books (including prequels and novellas) along with deleted scenes and series FAQ at https://kimmcdougall.com/valkyrie-bestiary.

BOOKS BY KIM MCDOUGALL

Valkyrie Bestiary Novels
Dragons Don't Eat Meat
Dervishes Don't Dance
Hell Hounds Don't Heel
Grimalkins Don't Purr
Kelpies Don't Fly
Ghouls Don't Scamper
Devils Don't Lie
Unicorns Don't Cry
Worlds Don't Collide

Valkyrie Bestiary Novellas
The Last Door to Underhill
The Girl Who Cried Banshee
Three Half Goats Gruff
Oh, Come All Ye Dragons
Thorn of Vioska

The Hidden Coven Series:
Inborn Magic
Soothed by Magic
Trigger Magic
Bellwether Magic
Gone Magic

Writing as Eliza Crowe
The Shifted Dreams Series:
Pick Your Monster
Lost Rogues

About the Author

If Kim McDougall could have one magical superpower, it would be to talk to animals. Or maybe to shift into animal form. Definitely, fantastical critters and magic often feature in her stories. So until she can change into a griffin and fly away, she writes dark paranormal action and epic fantasy tales, from her home in Quebec, Canada.

Visit Kim Online at KimMcDougall.com.